TO STEPH
ALL THE BEST
SCOTT IS AWESOME

MAIDSTONE

Lust, Murder, Greed, and a Cover Up in a Small New England Town

A Novel

By Marc Youngquist

Swamp Dog Hollow
PO Box 85
Middlefield, CT 06455

www.marcyoungquist.com

doghouse111@yahoo.com

Cover and internal artwork by Aleta Gudelski, www.aletagudelski.com

Geraldine Gormley, Senior Editor
Geoff Bottone, Executive Editor and layout and cover design

ISBN: 9781699892763

Chapter 1

February 9, 2010, was a typically cold night in Maidstone, a small village tucked into one of the valleys of the Berkshire Hills. The air was dry and crisp with a light dusting of new snow covering the ground. Traffic at 2 a.m. had all but stopped. On a Tuesday night everyone would be home in bed—there would be a few restaurant workers finishing up their late shift. Of course, there would be a couple of police officers watching over the town. Except for the occasional drunk driver or maybe a heart attack, not much was going to happen until the town woke up at dawn and things began to come alive.

It could seem boring to some, Danny Gilcrest didn't mind the quiet. It gave him a chance to catch up on his studies in a few community college courses, so he could move on to a four-year degree. He could do some research in the stock market even though he had very little to invest. This job had turned into a lot more than he had ever imagined. At times it was boring, just not all the time. The pay wasn't great, though it was okay. The bills were getting paid and there was more than enough for his daily expenses. He could go out any night he liked if he didn't go nuts and spend like he was one of the New York stock brokers who frequented the town.

Maidstone really did look like an Andrea Smythe painting with the new clean snow. Then again, this is the town that Smythe lived in and painted year after year. The recent dusting made it look just the way it should for a small, quiet New England town in the dead of winter.

The radio barked, "Unit 1, check-out a suspicious vehicle at the Shell Station on Route 9, just south of the Housatonic Inn. An unidentified caller has stated that he had driven by the place twice in the past hour, and the vehicle was still there idling."

Danny was almost happy to be interrupted and have something to do. Some of the guys on the midnight shift would go in the hole after the bars closed and catch a few hours of sleep, Danny couldn't do that. The first time he heard the term *going in the hole*, he had no idea what they were talking about. There was always some vacant estate with a long driveway that you could pull into, and no one would ever see you. There were also the seasonal places that were closed for months of the year that no one ever wandered into except the police who had keys to the gates to make routine checks. During his time in the service, Danny had often dug a hole to sleep in at night for protection; he didn't make the connection until it had been explained to him. After six years in the Marines, sleeping on duty was something he just couldn't do. Even if he wanted to, his body wouldn't let him.

Danny drove the mile or so to the gas station. He didn't recall seeing any vehicles in the area when he passed by earlier in the evening. This is a well-travelled route especially for patrol vehicles because it took them past most of businesses and shops that might be broken into. Then again, any of the drunks headed north from Great Barrington or travelling south from Lee would pass by there. This was

Maidstone's center of activity, if a few dozen cars could be called activity.

As he pulled up near the gas station, Danny took note that there were no tire tracks in the new snow. There were also no vehicles in the general area that looked like they had been running as they were all dusted with the new snow. He decided to exit his patrol vehicle and listen for the sound of an idling vehicle. Danny figured that the caller might have used the gas station as an identifiable location near where the vehicle was sitting.

"Dispatch, I will be out of the car at the Shell Station. I don't see the vehicle; I will be checking the area."

"Roger," was the response.

As he stepped out of the cruiser, he reached for his flashlight on the seat. Not knowing that he'd be standing on ice, he stepped out of the vehicle. As his weight came down, his foot shot straight forward into the door. He flipped out of the door coming down hard onto his back slamming his head into the pavement.

"What the hell!"

Chapter 2

Danny Gilcrest landed so hard on the snow-covered ground that there had been an audible boom as he struck the pavement. He was flat on his back, surprised, dazed, and hurting. The impact had knocked the wind out of him.

The sudden fall and not being able to breathe had spooked Danny, and he was trying to figure out just how badly he had injured himself. It had happened so fast that he couldn't remember slipping or falling. He could just remember hitting his head hard. One second, he was stepping from the cruiser and the next he was halfway under the vehicle, trying to figure out how he had gotten there.

Even now, the light dusting of snow hid the black ice. Danny was trying to get his wind back, and he began to think he wasn't hurt all that bad. He checked himself out and found he was able to move his toes and fingers. His head hurt like hell. His right leg was still inside the vehicle. His left leg was now under the cruiser, and his shin hurt from slamming into the door. He was going to have to untangle himself from a very awkward position.

After what seemed like an eternity, he tried to get up; his position made it a difficult maneuver. Adjusting his body, he noticed that he was covered in tiny chunks of ice. Strange, he thought; how on earth did that happen? He reached up and began to brush the ice off his chest. The ice wasn't moving; it was clinging to his coat. As he brushed harder, he realized his hand was stinging. He shook it to get the ice off.

In the dim light he could see that there were tiny cuts on his hand. Danny thought he saw blood. He couldn't make sense of the past few minutes and what was going on. He could just imagine how pissed the Chief was going to be if he went out on worker's comp for slipping on the ice and banging his head. Still catching his breath, he rolled to his side and pulled his leg out of the driver's side door. Slowly he pushed himself to his knees. Danny reached up to the door to help himself up on his unsteady legs and the slippery surface. That's when he noticed that his window was open. He couldn't remember opening it, and on such a cold night why would he?

Off in the distance near the old train station, Danny thought he heard a car start up. His hand was still stinging. When he held his hand up to the light, he could see there were dozens of tiny cuts oozing blood. As he listened to the sound of the engine down the road, he wondered how he had cut his hand falling out of the cruiser. Then he remembered hearing a boom and wondered just how hard had he hit the pavement? *Wait a minute*, he thought, *I must have hit the window on the way down and broke it. The Chief is going be pissed*. Danny slowly moved around the door to examine the damage, and sure enough the window had shattered in a million little pieces.

Porch lights from surrounding houses were coming on, and people were looking out their windows. Now what triggered this? He was more confused than ever.... No one in a house could have heard him fall.

In the background, Danny could hear a car heading south on Route 9 toward Great Barrington. It was so still and quiet that the engine noise stood out. Reaching into the vehicle to pick up the flashlight he had dropped, he caught sight of

7

his hand and the door. He noticed that the town seal on the door had holes in it. He shined the light across the rest of the surface and saw several more holes. He even stuck his finger in one to prove to himself that it was, in fact, a hole.

As he realized what had happened, Danny's reaction played out in slow motion. In one move, he dropped to a knee behind the door, drew his weapon and looked toward where the shot must have come from. He quickly scanned that area and didn't see any movement or anything out of the ordinary. Pulling his radio from its holster, Danny contacted Dispatch.

"Unit One to Dispatch, I think I've just been shot at."

"Unit One, say again," Dispatch responded.

"Dispatch, I think I've just been shot at. My location is the Shell Station on Route 9. I think the suspect vehicle headed south on Route 9 toward Great Barrington."

"What do you mean? You think you got shot at? Are you hit?"

"I'm not hit; at least I don't think I am. As I got out of the cruiser, I slipped and fell and that was when someone took a shot at me."

"So why do you think you were shot at?"

"Shit," was his reply. "There are a bunch of holes in my door, and my side window is shattered. I think I heard a boom as I hit the ground."

There was a long pause on the Dispatcher's side—too long. Before Dispatch could respond, Unit Two, Gary Carlson, came up on the air. "I am south bound and about two minutes out."

The next call was from the Sergeant in Dispatch again asking, "What do you mean, you think you were shot at?" The tone was questioning and a bit sarcastic.

Danny got back on the radio and started to explain the call to the gas station, the ice, the fall, the boom and, then he cut himself off. In a Marine Sergeant's voice that could be heard at the station without the use of a radio, he told him; "Get your ass down here and get me some help — someone just tried to kill me, you asshole."

The Desk Sergeant tried to pull rank. Unit Two cut him off and directed Dispatch to contact Great Barrington Police Department and the State Police and tell them that there had just been a shooting in Maidstone and that the intended victim was a police officer.

Soon Carlson arrived, and he and Danny moved off toward where he thought the suspect had been.

"Watch the trees!" Danny yelled, "That's where I think the shot came from, I am pretty sure he's long gone."

"Why do you think he's gone?" Carlson, asked

"Not too long after I fell, and hearing what I know now was the shot, I heard a vehicle start up down in the area of the train station. It headed south. I am guessing it was the getaway car."

Just to the south of the gas station, there was a stand of pine trees and shrubbery at the edge of Town Park Road. Behind this was a park that hadn't been plowed. Just south of West River Road, out in the area of the pines, they found compacted snow behind the low shrubbery and foot tracks leading to and from the location into the park. They followed the tracks which led them up the hill to Route 9 and then across the Housatonic River bridge.

"You're right," agreed Officer Carlson.

The foot prints led them to the old train station, where the prints ended, and a set of tire tracks headed up the driveway, out to Route 9 and turned south toward Great Barrington.

The old train station was now being used for town storage, while the Town Hall was being renovated. Since it wouldn't be open until 10 a.m., the town crew had not taken the time to plow the driveway. Near the footprints, the two officers found a cigarette butt with a brown filter on top of the snow. Further off they spotted a Styrofoam coffee cup several feet away from the tire tracks on top of the new snow. They made a mental note of the items that were out of place.

"It sounds like the cavalry is finally coming." Danny motioned in the direction of the sirens heading their way.

The first to arrive was the north patrol car from Great Barrington coming up Route 9.

"I didn't see any cars going south on 9," reported the Great Barrington officer.

Next, a unit from the State Police pulled in followed by Maidstone Police Department's Detective Lieutenant Snyder instead of the Shift Sergeant. At this time of the night, Snyder would've been fast asleep. It was remarkable that he was on the scene so quickly. His deep concern for his officer's plight went unnoticed, real deep concern.

Danny was glad to see someone in authority show up and take charge. He was too shaken to think straight plus his head was killing him. Although he really didn't care for Lieutenant Snyder and what he knew about him, Danny respected the rank, though he was having serious doubts about the Lieutenant—very serious doubts. There was something off about this guy. For a small town police department with little major crime he always appeared to be so busy: piles of paper-work on his desk' forever in a rush, preoccupied. His door was always closed and when he was away, even for just a cup of coffee from the break room the door was locked. Also there was the investigation of Penny's murder. His brief encounters with the Lieutenant had always left Danny wondering what the Lieutenant really meant when he said something. The murder investigation of Penny came to mind and whether any of it was true. Things in Maidstone for the most part were never that intense or frequent, unlike tonight.

Danny refocused as Lieutenant Snyder began to question him about what had happened. Before Danny could answer, the Lieutenant would interrupt with other questions.

"Are you sure you didn't see the suspect?"

"How come you didn't get a look at the car?"

"You were so close, how was that possible?"

"Are you sure there weren't any tire tracks at the gas station?"

The questions came fast and furious from Lieutenant Snyder. For the most part Danny never got to finish his statement. Then the State Trooper tried to get in on the interview. Lieutenant Snyder told him that Maidstone would handle the case and for the Trooper to try and locate the getaway vehicle.

The Trooper moved away, without being able to ask any questions so he couldn't relay information to other units searching for the suspect. All they had was the initial radio call to go on. If there was more information, Lieutenant Snyder was keeping it to himself. The State Trooper was looking for more details, and he was very frustrated that he was not getting any.

More units were arriving and no one was taking control of the scene. People were walking everywhere checking for a suspect that was long gone.

"Lieutenant, the scene is becoming compromised," said Danny.

"I will take care of that," Lieutenant Snyder replied. "Right now, we need to get you to a hospital to be checked out for a head injury." He made no effort to control the people wandering around. For Snyder the crimes scene was a minor problem. His biggest worry was that Danny was still alive.

"Don't worry, we have people on the way, and we will have the scene locked down shortly," the Lieutenant continued. "You may have been hurt worse than you think, and I don't want any crap from the union that we didn't take care of you."

An ambulance arrived, and Lieutenant Snyder walked Danny over to it and instructed the EMTs to take him to the hospital for a full evaluation. As they were closing the doors, Danny yelled, "Lieutenant, there is some evidence between the shooting location and where the getaway car was parked." Lieutenant Snyder nodded his head, and the EMT slammed the doors. Danny was about to protest and get out of the ambulance. There was so much more to tell. That is when they stuck the IV in his arm, and his thoughts went elsewhere.

Chapter 3

Lieutenant Snyder approached Officer Gary Carlson, the second unit on the scene, and asked, "What is this about evidence you guys found?"

Gary told him about the coffee cup and the cigarette butt that they had seen. He also mentioned the foot prints in the snow and the tire tracks at the train station. Gary headed off in that direction to show Lieutenant Snyder. Before he had taken a few steps, Lieutenant Snyder stopped him and told him that the investigators would take care of it and that he was needed out on Route 9 to direct traffic.

As one of the most junior officers, Gary obeyed Lieutenant Snyder's directive without question and headed for the road. Gary thought about how Lieutenant Snyder was second only to the Chief. It was sometimes hard to tell who out ranked whom. While the Chief was the number one man in the department, Lieutenant Snyder often operated very independently. Overheard conversations between them did not sound like a superior speaking to a subordinate. It was more like two equals having a conversation. At times, the subordinate sounded much more superior to the Chief. It was all very strange.

Not long after, a State Police Sergeant arrived and advised Lieutenant Snyder that the State Police Major Case Squad was on its way to process the scene. Lieutenant Snyder told the Sergeant that Major Case Squad had not been requested and that the Maidstone detectives would handle the scene.

The Sergeant was taken aback—it was routine for all major crime scenes, such as attempted murder, to be processed by the Major Case Squad.

The State Police Sergeant knew the track record of the Maidstone Police Department. One year ago, the department handled a murder case that the District Attorney was not too happy with it. Prior to that case the State Police Sergeant was aware of another major investigation which was over 15 years ago. In that case the State Police Major Case Squad was the lead investigators. The State Police Sergeant asked Lieutenant Snyder about it anyway.

"Lieutenant, about how many murders or attempted murders have you personally handled in Maidstone?"

"That was then; this is now. Maidstone will handle this scene."

The Sergeant couldn't make the Maidstone Police Department turn over their investigation to the Commonwealth, the District Attorney could. Lieutenant Snyder knew this, he just didn't care. During the time it would take to notify everyone and go through the proper channels and coordinate between the Chief and the District Attorney's Office, it would be all over. Lieutenant Snyder would have plenty of time to take care of all the loose ends and still have time for a coffee. He really didn't have much to do except wait. Without taking control and locking down the scene, chaos would take over. The crime scene would soon be completely compromised. Only a few details needed to be addressed, and Lieutenant Snyder knew they would be easy enough to handle. The one detail he couldn't fix was the fact that Danny Gilcrest was still alive.

14

Within minutes, Maidstone became a flurry of activity as Lieutenant Snyder expected. The closing of Route 9 in front of the gas station caused a major traffic jam. Everyone in town wanted to know what was going on. Word quickly spread, and news crews descended on the tiny New England town. There was not another news-worthy story west of Springfield. Everyone was heading to Maidstone as soon as they learned about the attempted murder of a police officer.

The State Police Major Case Squad had nearly made it to the scene when they were recalled. At 9 a.m., seven hours after the attack, the Major Case Squad was sent back to the scene. This time, they made it to the gas station only to find that dozens of people were already there. The Maidstone Police Department had started to process the scene. Detective Lieutenant Ronnie Cavanaugh of the State Police met up with Snyder. Snyder apologized for any misunderstanding and stated, "We have some evidence to turn over to the State Police. There are photographs of the scene that we need to give you. Once they are down-loaded with the proper notations we will send them along. Of course, we will turn over all reports to the State Police."

Lieutenant Cavanaugh knew something was wrong; he hadn't been told what. He was in on some of the earlier details just not the big picture. He knew that a call had come from the Commissioner's office to get down to Maidstone fast and to freeze the crime scene. By the time the Major Case Squad arrived, it was too late. There was nothing left to freeze. Whatever the Commissioner had been hoping to find was long gone. The scene had been walked over and even the shot-up police cruiser had been towed back to police headquarters. Lieutenant Cavanaugh knew how to process crime scenes, he couldn't figure out where to start with a mess like this. He stood looking at the jumble of people trying to figure out where to begin. All he could think was that if the mutt didn't confess, they had no case. Everything had been compromised. Lieutenant Cavanaugh made his way to the inn to call the Commissioner and break the bad news. In as calm and professional voice as he could, he explained the recall of the Major Case Squad when the call first came in. He relayed what he found when he got there seven hours later after they were sent back. The Commish didn't like bad news, and this couldn't be any worse. Here was an attempted murder of a police officer, and everything had turned to dog shit. Cavanaugh braced for the explosion he knew was coming. There was no explosion. Instead of a blast of four letter words, there was a calm understanding voice.

"That's okay, Ronnie," said the Commissioner. "Do what you can at the scene and document it as though it had not been compromised. When you get the evidence from the police department, follow your normal evidence gathering procedures. After you get the reports, make sure whoever made the report confirms that they are their reports. Process the reports like you would evidence. Tag it and bag it all. Got it?"

"Yes, sir," Lieutenant Cavanaugh replied, and the call abruptly ended.

He replaced the phone and was totally confused by the events of the past few hours. The scene had been trashed. The Commish had personally ordered his team down there to salvage a situation that was beyond saving. Now, when the Commish heard the bad news, he wasn't even upset. In the past, he was known to send a telephone into orbit when something like this happened—not this time. It was almost like he had expected this. *What the hell?*

Chapter 4

From August 2001 to July 2007 the Marines were great, maybe even beyond great. Where could you exercise for several hours a day, go for long walks through the woods, shoot all kinds of neat weapons day and night and go all over the world and get paid for it? There were, of course, a few down sides to being a Marine—not the least of which was that almost everyone in the Company had one or more Purple Hearts.

Now it was time to decide: stay in or move on. The Retention NCO wanted to keep Danny in when his six-year enlistment expired. The Marines were ready to offer him just about anything as an incentive plus a cash bonus. Danny wanted some place warm, though not too warm and maybe a nice beach somewhere.

"I have just the place for you," the Retention NCO said, "Hawaii."

"Hawaii, really," Danny countered.

"Sure. The Brigade is stationed at Kaneohe Marine Corps Air Station on the opposite side of Oahu from Waikiki." The retention NCO figured he had him and was pulling out the paperwork to do a re-enlistment.

Danny had almost six years in and knew one thing about the Marines: wherever you were stationed, you were almost never there. The Marines were always on the way somewhere.

"Where is the Brigade now?" Danny asked.

"Hawaii that's their home station," was the quick reply.

"When do they deploy?" asked Danny.

"What do you mean?" asked the Retention NCO, knowing that this re-enlistment wasn't going to happen if he answered the question.

"You know, how long before the Brigade departs from Hawaii to go to some exotic place," asked Danny.

"Oh, they're not going to Iraq or Afghanistan," said the Retention NCO.

"Fine," said Danny. "So where are they going?"

"Korea, for cold weather training," was the quiet reply, hoping Danny didn't hear him.

Bob Marshall School of Forestry was looking better by the minute.

"See ya, I'm outta here," and so ended six years in the Marines.

Chapter 5

Forestry School was just what Danny wanted. He would be outside, just not in every type of weather twenty-four hours a day. The school offered a certificate in land surveying where he would have a better chance of landing a higher paying job. He wouldn't be a millionaire. He would be doing something he enjoyed and have a few bucks to spend. After being a Marine, it wouldn't be as exciting or as challenging-- it would be a good life. He would have time to fish, hike, and camp out in nice weather, with the emphasis on *nice.* He could now pick the days to go out in the woods. If things looked bad, he wouldn't have to go. He loved his time out in the mountains. With the Marines, suffering does build character—he had enough character at that point for several people to share. The school required several high school math and English courses with a grade of "B" or better. Danny was a little behind in that area. He had passed all the courses, unfortunately not all with a "B," and one or two were still lacking. Danny never knew how important math was until he started plotting locations on a map, calling for indirect fire and planning load lists for helicopters. He learned fast, the problem was if it wasn't on his high school transcript, it didn't exist.

The forestry school had encouraged him to attend a local community college to get the required courses under his belt and then to apply. Bob Marshall pretty much guaranteed him a spot in the school plus they were sure they could find him a part-time job to help him through. The GI Bill would cover most of his expenses. There was a veteran's house on campus where he could stay. It was designed for returning veterans with no savings to have a chance at a college education without having to take out large student loans. It sounded like a plan. So, in September of 2007 Danny started the fall semester at the community college down in Great Barrington.

He moved back to his hometown of Maidstone and took a job at the local hardware store where he knew the owner. He never worked in a hardware store and wasn't a plumber or a carpenter. This wasn't a problem with the customers who knew what they wanted, now the New York and New Jersey weekenders were clueless. They needed help to find a widget to fix the thing-a-majig that is under the sink off to the right and is real shiny. One day a guy came in looking for carriage bolts. Danny knew there were a lot of people with horses in town. Some had wagons and carriages and drove teams of horses. He didn't think that the hardware store would carry that specialty item. He suggested that the guy go to a store that sold carriages or go online and see what was available. The customer starred at Danny trying to determine if he was kidding or not. When he realized that Danny was serious, the customer located the owner and explained the recent conversation he had with Danny. All the owner could do was shake his head. In the end the bolts were in the bin where they had been on display since the store opened 150 years ago. Danny was then given a catalog with all the different nuts, bolts, screws, washers, nails, etc. and told to read and memorize the catalog. Working in the hardware store was frustrating, boring, and didn't pay much. So, when he heard about an arborist that was looking for someone to climb trees, he thanked the store owner and moved on. Truth be told, the store owner was about to suggest a career change back to the Marines for Danny.

Tree climbing was hard outdoor work. It was something he could understand, enjoy, and the pay was better and he still had his nights off to go to school. Berkshire Community College was just down the road in Great Barrington, and the courses were not all that difficult. He just had to complete the required semesters to qualify for Bob Marshall. In a year and a half, give or take, he would be off to New York State and a career in the woods. Until then he had a used Jeep and lived in a nice two-room apartment in a converted barn with a big old yellow Labrador that smiled. Now this wasn't your typical farm barn. Yes, there were horses, but the stalls were as nice and, in some cases, nicer than most people's houses. Danny was in one of the caretakers' apartments. For just two rooms, it had nearly 650 square feet of living space. There was one large room with an eat-in kitchen and the living area on the opposite wall. The bedroom could hold a king size bed, and just off the bedroom was the ¾ bathroom. This was more than enough for Danny, plus the place came furnished. The tables and chairs were hand-me-downs, but they were far from being junk. When the lady of the estate decided to redecorate the main house, the items that were no longer needed were moved into the caretaker's apartments. Everything was top shelf and showed hardly any wear. If it had shown any type of damage it would've been donated to some charity. One young lady who had visited Danny's barn said it was "Mission Style" furniture. Danny had been on numerous "missions" he just couldn't make the connection to that and the furniture. For very little money he had a place to stay, which was light years beyond his Marine Corps days even when he was stationed

21

stateside. In exchange, he had to do a little lawn mowing in the summer, rake the leaves in the fall, and do some snow shoveling in the winter for the main house. Most of the work was done by a hired landscaping company with Danny doing small things that had accumulated between their visits. Such a deal! Just twenty-five years old and living on estate in the Berkshires. Granted it wasn't his estate. Now between the apartment in Manhattan, the condo in Vail and the house in Marathon Key, the owners were seldom there not to mention the travel to Europe and other overseas destinations. Everything was going fine until one of the local police officers spotted him doing tree work. Gary Carlson, one of his buddies from high school stopped to catch up on what everyone was doing since graduation. Danny told him about his plans and that the tree work was just a bridge until he got into Bob Marshall.

Gary said, "Ya know, the police department is looking for reserve officers. If you came on the police department part-time, you could still do tree work go to school, … and the police department pays something towards college for fulltime and reserve officers."

"Well," Danny replied, "I wore a uniform for six years and took orders, good and bad. I think at this point I prefer to climb trees and leave it at that."

"Suit yourself," said Gary, "just remember tree work in the winter sucks, and the police department is not the big city. The worst thing that happens is some guy from The Big Apple has too many martinis at the Black Dog and has to be escorted out. This is a please and thank you police department."

"What?" asked Danny?

"You know, when you do a traffic stop you have to say, 'I am sorry, sir, you were clocked at 75 in a 30 zone. May I please see you license, registration and insurance card? Sir, would you please stay in your car, and I will process your ticket as quickly as possible so that I do not delay you any longer than is necessary.' We have to kiss everyone's ass because they are all doctors or attorneys or some other filthy rich type. If we are not polite, we get sued, and the chief gets pissed."

Danny thought about that for a moment and then replied, "I was a Marine for six years and a Sergeant for the last three years of my enlistment. I don't think I would fit in, thanks for thinking of me."

Danny put the thought of being a police officer behind him, though not for long. Tree climbing was fun, challenging, outside, and paid okay. There were almost always a few hours of overtime every week. That is until the work dried up and the layoff notices came out. In the spring time, all the out of towners are desperate to get their homes in order for the summer. The winter months brought a lot of damage so there is a lot of work. Spring spraying comes into play then the work drops way off, and the new guys get pink slips. In August of 2008 Danny's plan, simple as it was, had started to quickly fall apart.

Plan B: a phone call was made. "Hey, Gary is the police department still hiring?"

"Well, yah," came the response, "why the change of heart?"

"I need a job," Danny confessed. "I got laid off."

And so, started the Law Enforcement career of Danny Gilcrest, all by accident. The first step in one of many that could get him killed in a quiet New England Town.

Chapter 6

Reserve Officer training took place several nights a week and included other officers from nearby towns. It was a long, drawn-out process. Danny would still be a sworn officer in the Commonwealth of Massachusetts, just like if he had been through the regular police academy. The small towns of the Berkshires didn't need large police departments as the population and crime rate were both very low. The summer and fall months brought in all the tourists and the summer residents. Tanglewood up in Lenox would see huge concerts every week. Traffic after the events was a nightmare. Events at the Andrea Smythe Gallery could draw several hundred to a thousand people, all of whom wanted to get back to their inns or getaway homes as soon as the event ended. Reserve officers supplemented the full timers on traffic duty and coordinated parking. There wasn't any heavy lifting—just a lot of flapping of the arms directing traffic. The check came every week on time, and it was at a higher rate than climbing trees. There was also the small though appreciated stipend from the town for attending college. The town would cover all books plus $100 a month as long as the course was completed with a grade of "B" or better.

Danny was back on track—a few semesters of classes, a year or two of flapping arms, a small comfortable apartment, and the Jeep was still running: life is good.

The Housatonic Inn is a classy place. Danny liked stopping in and hanging out with the city types. However, it was a bit pricy, and he really didn't fit in. Meeting a nice young lady there was a distinct possibility. Unfortunately, once they found out he was a part-time police officer going to school nights and living in a barn, it kind of put the brakes on things.

As conversations would go, the same things would come up.

"What, no BMW?"

"You drive a 10-year-old Jeep Wrangler?"

"You live in a barn, seriously?"

About this time little dolly dimples would ask where the ladies' room was and exit, stage left.

Now heading down to the Butternut Brewery was a different story. Lots of locals plus hikers and skiers liked the place. The conversations would take a different tone.

"What do you drive?"

Danny would reply, "A Jeep Wrangler."

"Oh, cool," would be the response. "Soft top, I hope."

"Of course."

"Is the top down?" she would ask.

"The snow is gone, so of course the top is down," he would reply.

"Can we go for a ride?"

"Why sure we can, now there is someone who has to come with us."

This would bring a real look of disappointment and concern. "Who would that be?"

"My yellow Lab, Bear. He has been inside for a few hours, and I really need to let him out. Bear loves going for a

ride with the top down. Don't worry, you get to sit in the front seat," Danny would say.

This would bring a huge smile to just about any young lady. If it didn't, then it was time for Danny to move on. If she didn't like Wranglers and Labradors she probably wasn't going to like him—who needs her if she is that way.

As they headed out the door to the Wrangler, the question would come up, "Where do you live?"

The practiced response would be, "In a barn."

The reply was almost always, "How cool."

26

This would usually be followed by a hike up Butternut Basin or maybe a walk to the Ledges to watch the sunset. The view from Monument Mountain looked a little different every few weeks. So, it never got boring. Either way it was outside, enjoyable, and, well, cheap. Danny would then offer to cook dinner which was almost always met with extreme skepticism as he did not look or sound like one of the TV chefs. He assured them that if they didn't like his cooking, they could always get a pizza; that was never the case. Danny had an easy meal that could be ready in short order without a lot of preparation.

While the young lady was enjoying the view of the estate with a glass of wine and the complete attention of Bear, Danny would be busy in the kitchen. Having Bear as a wingman was great. He could keep a young lady entertained for hours. When you told him to go lay down, he reluctantly did.

Dinner would be Rock Cornish games hens with long grain and wild rice and glazed carrots. There would be a slight orange glaze to the hens and a touch of brown sugar on the carrots to sweeten them up just a bit. It wasn't very creative, and looked way more impressive than a pizza and it would be served on a beautiful farm estate in the Berkshires by a former Marine with a yellow Labrador.

Who knew that an old Jeep Wrangler, a Labrador retriever, and barn could get you a date?

Danny learned not to question it and just go with the flow.

Once again life and a plan were back on track, plan "B" was working. Now how was he going to be able to transition all this to Saranac Lake?

Chapter 7

Joe Banzano, "Joey B," loved the Town of Maidstone. He also loved to eat, drink beer, smoke cigarettes and watch sports on TV as long as he had complete control of the remote. His idea of strenuous physical activity bounced between cutting his toe nails and doing laps to the refrigerator for a cold Bud. Joe was too cheap to give a tip for pizza delivery, so he figured running out for a pizza would be good exercise to stay in shape. He also loved being a Maidstone police officer. He would ride around in a cruiser with the heater on full bore in the winter and the AC cranked up in the summer. Joe could listen on the radio to the Sox, Bruins, Celtics or the Patriots and be almost assured of no interruptions. If directing traffic needed to be done and he had to get out of the cruiser, there was almost always a reserve officer he could call on to get the job done. One of the unstated requirements of a reserve officer was that they were expected to donate time to the department for free. It was considered on-the-job training. Or more realistically, you have to give up some time if you want to come on full time. Either way, it worked for Joe—that is until the afternoon he got a bad case of indigestion. Joe had just finished a meatball sub with extra cheese and 32 oz. Pepsi at Sandy's Deli. He headed over to the Rite Aid Pharmacy in Lee and picked up some Rolaids and wolfed down a handful. The pharmacist came out from behind the counter and took one look at Joe and offered him a chair. Joe declined. The pharmacist insisted and began interrogating him. Joe didn't look very good—not good at all.

"How do you feel?" the pharmacist asked. "Do you have pressure on your chest? Does your left arm or jaw hurt? How is your breathing? When was the last time you saw a doctor?"

The answers weren't good. In just a few short minutes the color in Joe's face had turned to an ashen blue and his breathing became more labored. It wasn't a very warm day; still sweat was soaking through his grey uniform shirt leaving dark blotches.

"Call 911," the pharmacist told the clerk. "I think Joe is having a heart attack."

EMTs, the Fire Department, and several police officers arrived. Joe was transported down to the hospital in Great Barrington where he was stabilized then air lifted to Bay State Medical in Springfield. Joe survived, went on a diet, and quit smoking. His time in law enforcement was over. The damage was done, and there would not be a complete recovery from the long-term effects of a poor life style. Part of his heart muscle no longer functioned. He was going to survive. For him, his cops and robber days were now a thing of the past.

The call went out to the reserve officers in Maidstone: we have a full-time opening. And so, the accidental journey for Danny Gilcrest continued with one more step in a long path to a shotgun blast.

Chapter 8

Danny got one of the first calls. A lot of the reserve officers were older and had full-time jobs that paid better than being a police officer. They were reserve officers because they liked the extra pay and the status of being a police officer, even if it was only part time. Some worked construction, one was a teacher with summers off, there was an electrician, and two were property managers. None really wanted to do the job full time. By the same token, it did not take much convincing to get Danny to apply. He could still go to school and work towards getting into Bob Marshall. He could take courses locally that could go towards his degree and certification in forestry and land surveying. He didn't have to give up his dream or be a small-town police officer for the rest of his life. This would just be a great bridge job/temporary career on his way to Saranac Lake and the woods that he loved. It also paid better than part-time, and there were benefits which he hoped he would never use except for the paid vacation.

So, on a late summer day, Danny Gilcrest raised his right hand once more and promised to protect and defend the citizens of the Town of Maidstone in the Commonwealth of Massachusetts, to obey the Constitution of the United States and the laws of the Commonwealth and Ordinances of the Town of Maidstone.

It was a smaller responsibility than the last time he swore an oath. It was no less significant. He was sure he made a good decision, no, a great decision. Everything seemed to be breaking his way. The Marines hadn't killed him, he had a full-time job, he was on his way to a college education, and he had a great dog. Life is good.

Danny was right; his life was good — for two other people in town, not so much.

No one knows what goes on behind closed doors, or so they say. There are always people who love to throw doors wide open and speak damaging things, hurtful things, true enough, though still hurtful.

There are some relationships that start off good then end badly. There are other relationships that start off bad and only get worse. Then there are relationships that start off bad, get worse and try some new experiment to get things back on track that was never on track in the first place. Anyone with half a brain can predict that this will not end well and in most cases, they don't. Nasty divorces are common with former lovers' fighting over who gets the house, the kids, the family pet, weird Uncle Harold's desk. The next step is which friends you take with you after the divorce. Most of the time one of the spouses doesn't end up dead.

Nothing ever happens in Maidstone, well, most of the time.

Chapter 9

Gary had lied—well, maybe not a full out-and-out lie. He just didn't tell the whole truth. Things did happen in Maidstone. Not the constant inner-city things, like Springfield or Boston, just things that kept a small-town police officer hopping. Maidstone has a small permanent population, it also has the transients. There are the tourists and the summer and vacation people. They can double and triple the population in a weekend. And these well-off people require help in many forms, landscapers, maids, restaurant workers, handymen, chefs, bartenders, actors, and stagehands, you name it. All these people migrate to the Berkshires every summer to fill those service positions and make a stay in the Berkshires a quality and enjoyable experience.

Unfortunately, as the population soars, problems do too. The police on the road are the first to go on every call, even those that might not seem law-enforcement related. There are the medical emergencies, fires, anyone who needs help of any kind and, of course, accidents. The police respond immediately; volunteers who respond take time to get there. Then there are problems that end up in Maidstone even though they didn't start in Maidstone. Things could happen up in Lenox, Pittsfield or come off the Mass Pike and end up in the quiet New England town.

In his first two weeks on the job, Danny was involved in a high-speed chase of a stolen car. Then there was a fatal motor-vehicle accident plus a suicide—not what you'd expect for a small-town police officer.

Danny had been working the 6 p.m. to 2 a.m. shift when the call came over the radio.

"All units, Lenox PD has spotted a stolen vehicle heading south on Route 9 travelling at a high rate of speed. Lenox lost contact with the vehicle about a mile north of the Maidstone line in Lee."

Danny took a post opposite the Housatonic Inn; and Gary Carlson, the north patrol vehicle, was a bit further up Route 9.

The excited voice of Carlson came over the radio.

"In pursuit south bound, the vehicle is not stopping."

Danny maneuvered his vehicle out into the road. As he positioned the vehicle in the intersection, he spotted the headlights far off in the distance. At this point Danny had the cruiser blacked out with no lights on. There was no time to deploy the stop-sticks. The pursuing cruiser was well back and not gaining on the stolen motor vehicle. Danny waited until the vehicle was about 300 yards away before he turned everything on. The stolen vehicle attempted to brake and swerved, striking the curb and flattening the passenger's side tire. The car spun out, and the two occupants bolted from the vehicle. Unfortunately for the driver, he wasn't doing a real fast get-a-way trying to get out without undoing his seatbelt. This bought Gary just enough time to pull up and exit his vehicle. He made a body slam to the suspect as he tried to run away into the darkness. Danny took off into the pitch black after running man number two. They left the Main Street area and ran behind the Bond and Bradley Center and kept heading west behind some houses. Fortunately, at this time of night, all the doors at the center would be closed and locked. The suspect couldn't disappear into one of the buildings that made up the campus.

Danny soon lost sight of the suspect in the darkened back streets and yards, and continued on in a straight line figuring that the suspect would try and put the most distance between himself and the stolen car. After a few hundred yards, Danny slowed his dead run to a slow jog. More importantly, he listened. He waited for the sound of the suspect crashing into things in the dark and the noise of running and heavy breathing. He heard nothing. Danny slowly moved forward in the same direction, and this time he heard thump followed by a muffled, "Oh shit."

Slowly Danny moved forward, weapon drawn in a low, ready position. The night was quiet with no wind to cover any noise. The slightest sounds could be heard at a great distance. Then Danny heard the crunch of footsteps on gravel—white pea gravel to be exact and he remembered the times walking in the cemetery across from the Congregational Church on Main Street.

Danny went into a stalking mode, slowly moving forward, scanning from side to side, using his eyes and ears trying to detect a sound or movement. If anyone had seen Danny at this point, they would have been wondering why in the world he had such a strange look on his face. Danny had his mouth open in a wide oval shape and his lower jaw tilted forward at a slight angle. While it looked strange, it served two purposes. First it allowed him to breathe unrestricted through his mouth. This cut his breathing sounds almost down to nothing even after his hard run to overtake the suspect. Secondly, the open mouth and jaw tilt allowed the ear canals to open up just a bit more so that he could hear better. He looked like a hooked trout; it worked, so screw it. After a few yards, he could hear heavy breathing. Danny eased up towards the sound. When he felt he was close, he turned on his flashlight, illuminating suspect number two. He flashed the light on just long enough to blind the suspect and destroy his night vision. For that split second, Danny kept his eyes closed and looked away. With the suspect now surprised and distracted, Danny moved in.

"Freeze," Danny yelled.

"What's the problem, Officer?" was the calm questioning response. "What's with the light?"

"Put your hands up and get on the ground," Danny commanded.

"For what, I'm only out for a walk. What's with the gun?" the suspect demanded.

This guy was trying to convince him that he was just out for a walk behind someone's house and then in a cemetery at 1 a.m. Danny moved forward all the while ordering the suspect to put up his hands and get on the ground. The suspect continued to plead ignorance as to why in the world the police were yelling at him. Danny could see that he had nothing in his hands and advanced on the suspect who was still trying to play the innocent bystander. Here was Danny with a few hundred headstones witnessing one of the greatest performances ever. Even the dead could not believe what they were hearing. In one swift moved, Danny holstered his weapon, slammed his right forearm into the suspect's chest, and kicked his legs out from under him. In the next instant before the suspect could react, Danny flipped him over on his

36

stomach and put the cuffs on him. A search didn't produce any weapons or drugs that Danny figured had to be there. In fact, the suspect didn't have anything on him, not even a wallet or change. Danny led him back to the cruiser. The suspect demanded he be released because he hadn't done anything except go for a walk. In the street light, Danny could see that the suspect was sweating heavily and had grass stains on the knees of his trousers.

He placed the suspect in the rear of his vehicle while he continued to protest that he was just out for a walk. He was going to sue for false arrest, and he would have Danny's badge. In one final demand, the suspect wanted to know, "What are you arresting me for?"

Danny's quick reply, "Reckless parking in a disorderly car."

A stunned look came over the suspect; his mouth dropped open, it quickly changed. "Thank you, officer. I am soon to be a millionaire, this is a false arrest, and there is no such charge. I demand that you immediately release me."

"You have the right to remain silent," stated Danny. "Please do so," and slammed the door shut.

Danny walked over to the North Patrol. "Your guy talking?" Danny asked.

"No, I nailed him good coming out of the car, and he isn't a happy camper. He has a bunch of cuts and scrapes from hitting the pavement. He's claiming excessive use of force and is demanding that I release him immediately or he is going to sue, have my badge, you know the drill. What's your guy's name?" asked Gary.

"No idea," said Danny. "We haven't gotten past the false arrest. He was only out for a walk, and, like you, my job is on the line. Who knew we would find not one, but two lawyers out this time of night."

"Well," Carlson said, "His name just might be Fredrick Terwilliger."

"If your guy isn't talking, then how did you come by that name?" asked Danny.

"Your Mensa Society candidate left his wallet in the stolen car. The driver's license looks like your guy".

"Well then," Danny said, "time to get a confession and a spontaneous utterance from Mr. Terwilliger. I don't think a judge would believe that he was just out for a walk. Just to be safe let's tie up that possible loose end and be done with this. I heard that the Supervising District Attorney Marvin Cohen likes everything cut and dried."

Danny returned to his patrol vehicle and opened the rear door where the prisoner was sitting. He was greeted with more of the same concerning law suits, badges, jobs and making the innocent person an instant millionaire. This was going to be better than hitting the lottery. Danny let him go on and then interrupted him. "Look, Freddy boy, your buddy there just gave you up. He said that it was your idea to take the car. He's putting this all on you. Talk about getting thrown under the bus, your friend is no friend of yours. He wants to cut a deal and let the district attorney know he's fully cooperating. So, Mr. Terwilliger what do you want to do?"

"Son of a bitch," the suspect shot back. "It was his idea. I was ready to walk home when he spotted the car at the gas station with the engine running. He said that we would just use it to get home and then dump it. We'd only have it a few minutes, and there are never any cops around. It was all his idea," was the lame response.

"Well," asked Danny, "how's that short ride working out for you now?" He slammed the door closed.

"Just another quiet night in Maidstone," Gary Carlson commented.

"Yah," said Danny, "you know I would like to think we catch these guys because we're so good. Instead we catch these guys because they're so dumb."

As Gary walked back to his cruiser, he called out over his shoulder, "It still goes down in the "W" column."

It was a quiet ride to the station. The two were processed and turned over to Lenox PD for the original charges of theft of a motor vehicle. There wouldn't be a trial. The district attorney had enough to get them into a plea bargain deal and dispose of the case. The district attorney liked it when a suspect gave themselves up that way. After that it would be, "Here's the deal, take it or leave it." Hopefully the two mutts would realize that they had not gotten one number for the lottery that night and take the deal. Judges did not like it when guilty defendants took up valuable court time when the only result was going to be a conviction in the end. If they wanted a trial, they could have one. Then they would get some serious time, double what they would have gotten if they had taken the plea. The judge was not on the side of the district attorney. If you wanted to take up the court's time, then you would have to pay for it. Judges want to sort out the facts of a real case, not listen to a couple of losers who watched too many TV courtroom dramas.

Chapter 10

Danny's college courses were moving along at a steady pace. Granted it was a slow pace, still, it was steady. Not all the courses were available every semester, so the plan had to be spread out. One day Danny was talking to his Veteran's Counselor about his next course. Being a fellow Vet, the Counselor was always trying to help guys out and get them the best deal possible.

"Danny," the counselor said, "you can actually make money going to school if you want to take two more courses a semester."

"How's that?" asked Danny as he eased himself into the chair in front of his VA man? Making money going to school sounded like a great idea. It also sounded too good to be true and possibly might be illegal.

The Counselor reached into Danny's file and pulled out some paperwork.

"I know your plan is to go to Bob Marshall up in Saranac Lake, and you are taking the required prerequisites to get in. You're taking only one course a semester. If you up that to three courses a semester, you would become a ¾ time student. At that point the GI Bill would give you more money. More courses, more money—I wouldn't suggest more than three. You just don't have the time to spend on courses, work for the police department, manage to sleep, and have some fun. The town is kicking in some bucks, and there is the federal grant. There are scholarships for veterans, and additional scholarships for Marine veterans from the Marine Corps League. With a little effort you could have the entire cost of going to college paid for through these grants and scholarships and put the GI Bill portion in your pocket."

"That sounds great; the thing is I only need those few courses to get in to Bob Marshall. I really don't need the extra courses," said Danny.

"Au contraire, mon frère, in the long run, you do need them," the Counselor pointed out. "If you are here or at Bob Marshall, schools require you to take a certain number of standard courses. Right now, you are concentrating on advanced high school courses to meet the entrance requirements. Those are not going to be counted as part of your degree. During the two or more years that you attend Bob Marshall, they are going to have you take a few courses not related to forestry or surveying. You'll need required courses in English, biology, math, and several elective courses to balance out your education. We can check with Bob Marshall and find out which ones they will accept as transfer credits. If you do that, you get them out of the way before you get there. You will have a lighter load each semester. You can also take some of the easier electives mixed in with the mandatory courses that will not be as hard to pass. The other plus is that we are a community college, and the cost per class is less than half of what Bob Marshall is going to charge you. As an added bonus, if you take some of the criminal justice courses, you will be ahead of the game at the police department. You will have an advantage in any promotions. Once again, don't forget the money. This is a win, win for you. Actually, it is more like a win, win, win, homerun. "

41

Danny sat back in the chair. He didn't want to take more on now, everything the Counselor was saying made sense. The money would be nice of course, and having courses out of the way before he got to Bob Marshall sounded even better. He wasn't interested in promotions at the police department as that almost never happened. Besides he wasn't going to be there that long anyway. He realized that he had run into some situations that he was never trained for in the reserve police academy. There was this vacuum of knowledge for the job that had not been filled. He hated it when he would run into something he did not have the answer for. In police work, that was happening too often.

With some reluctance, Danny agreed to sign up. The more he thought about it the more it he realized that if he were going to get paid to go to school then he could turn down the extra duty traffic jobs and still have that extra income. Traffic duty wasn't hard, it was boring. Standing around for hours flapping your arms at traffic and somehow always finding one person who didn't think you were doing it right happened too often. As he worked out the details, he found that he would actually be making more money going to school than out on the street. It would take up about the same amount of time. Instead of standing on a dusty road he would be sitting in an air-conditioned classroom or in the winter a heated one, not standing outside in all kinds of weather. It sounded too good to pass up.

As Danny headed back to Maidstone, he went through the numbers in his head. He had started at the hardware store at minimum wage and then got a good bump up when he went to climbing trees and picking up some overtime. The pink slip came along; and instead of dropping back to minimum wage, he got his cop job making more money than he had ever dreamed of. The Counselor who found the funding for him had added four hundred and twenty three dollars of tax free money per month to Danny's income. He pulled over and wrote the numbers down and rechecked them twice. He never dreamed he would be making that much money so soon after getting out of the Marines. He figured he wouldn't see that kind of cash until he graduated from college and landed a real job. Here it was just falling in place. Life is good, Danny thought, very good. Danny looked up and noticed that he had stopped in front of the high school. "IF" he had done better in high school none of this would have happened.

How could he know that this would be the next step he would take that would lead to someone trying to kill him? College and a higher education could prove to be deadly, go figure. Now that was still down the road.

Chapter 11

It was going to be his fourth semester at the community college. He was taking three courses, trying to balance a heavy course with a light course. He would then take a course that he would find interesting and not require a lot of studying. If it did require studying, he wanted something that would not be a burden.

He stopped in to see the Curriculum Advisor to go over what was being offered, and explain to him what he wanted to do. The Director thought it was a good course of action.

"How about some criminal justice courses?" the Advisor suggested. "You're already a police officer and have the basics of the police academy to fall back on. Whatever course you take, you will already have a foundation of knowledge to build on. You will be ahead of those students who have not had any exposure to the criminal justice system."

That sounded like a plan to Danny. Most of the police academy courses were comparable to freshman college courses.

"I think I can handle that. What courses do you have available?"

"The one that jumps out at me is Criminal Investigation and the Presentation of Evidence." The Professor is the local District Attorney for Berkshire County, Marvin Cohen. It won't be a bad thing to have direct contact with him. On the plus side, you will see how he wants things done which can be beneficial in the long run for a police officer."

Danny thought about the Advisor's suggestion. He wasn't planning on being police officer forever. As far as a career option, it was more than he needed. On the other hand, the VA was putting money in his pocket and the course was going to be free, so why not?

"Sign me up."

And so, the journey continued on its slow and winding course. Unknown to Danny or anyone else, he had taken the next step on the road to getting shot at. How in the world could getting a free college education get a person killed? Joining the Marines could, he knew that was a given going in. Everyone understood that about the Marines, so how could college end up being a deadly choice?

Saturdays in the summer were always interesting. Without trying too hard you could find something going on in town. This Saturday had the entire Main Street tied up. It was a cross between a cruise night and a classic car show. Main Street was lined with every type of motor transportation. There were the muscle cars of the 60s and 70s, and there were classics including Model As and sports cars. There were MGAs, Aston Martins, Drop Head Jags, Austin Healy's, you name it. They were there, several hundred of them, and hordes of people. Only the vehicles on display were allowed to park on Main Street and the adjacent side streets. The people attending had to be bused in from off-site parking lots. Danny's job, along with the rest of the department, was to keep the traffic flowing. No one, not even the Chief, had the day off. While this was a big event for Maidstone, all the thru traffic of a summer day kept right on coming. Along with the cars, there were the street venders selling food, tee shirts, vehicle parts, and anything thing else even remotely associated with cars. The local merchants did okay sales wise. Now it was the town that made the big bucks charging for vendor space and permits.

As Danny came on duty, he heard one of the strangest broadcasts come over the radio. The inter-agency hotline used by all the adjoining departments was on the lookout for an armed robber.

The state police were looking for a suspect that had just robbed a toll booth. It was strange in two ways. First, whoever heard of robbing a toll taker? Second thing that stood out was the voice of the state trooper making the broadcast. It was almost a mechanical voice devoid of urgency and never changing in tone or inflection, dry, crisp, electronic sounding. The downside was that there was very little detail in the information.

"State Police on the hotline," stated the monotone voice. "Wanted for armed robbery of the Lee Toll—a white male driving a white van. Last seen west bound from the toll headed toward New York. It has been reported to have exited the highway."

Just the facts ma'am, just the facts. Not one extra word in the broadcast.

No marker, no age, no make on the vehicle, just bare facts. *Very professional sounding*, Danny thought. No excitement to cloud the broadcast. Kind of like the real old Adam 12 TV show. Most dispatchers get excited when they get a serious call and could not conceal it when they get on the radio. Not this guy. He was all business; he should be teaching dispatcher classes.

Danny made some brief notes based on the limited information and headed to his cruiser for several hours of traffic duty. The guy was west bound away from Lee and probably headed to New York State or the Pittsfield area. He won't be coming this way. Just in case, Danny tucked the 12-gauge shotgun into the scabbard that hung from the front seat. *You never know.*

Traffic was moving along slowly. Danny helped out with directing people pulling in and out of parking spots and telling people with brand new Mercedes SUVs and Range Rovers that they could not park on Main Street. There were signs all over the place advising everyone that Main Street was for display vehicles only and directing people to the off-site parking areas. There were always a few who couldn't read or figured that they were the exception — that the signs were for *"other"* people. Somewhat put out, they insisted that they could park there followed by the *"Do you know who I am?"* question. For the most part, Danny had no clue who these people were. He was polite and repeatedly explained why the people could not park their personal tanks on Main Street and would have to ride a school bus to the event. Fortunately for Danny, he had a "pit-bull" for backup who wouldn't take any guff from these self-important people. Money and big vehicles and who they were was of no concern to the Director of the event. She was in charge and no one had better cross her if they knew what was good for them. It was nothing to berate a young police officer in uniform that didn't make as much in a year as these people might spend on a good weekend in Vail. Just don't cross swords with the head of the Maidstone Historical Society, or you would get an ear full. Five feet two, 110 pounds grey haired, and somewhere in the area of 90 years old, and she wasn't taking shit from anyone. For Danny it was great to have a wingman with an attitude. Who was going to complain that a little old lady yelled at them? And a wingman she really was. Her family didn't come from old money, they came from ancient money. Railroads and granite quarrying in Vermont, Danny had heard. The family was also very military oriented as just about everyone in the family had served. Vivian had done her part as a transport pilot in World War II ferrying B-24 Bombers to airfields across the country and flying C-47s loaded with cargo destined for the war. That is where she met her husband who was a Marine Corps aviator flying Corsairs. Her husband was recalled to active duty flying Panther jets in Korea. For a time, her husband, Frank, had flown with John Glenn and Ted Williams. The family was die-hard Red Sox fans. Frank, full name Franklin Joseph Brennen, Esquire, had also managed to go fly fishing with Williams at the White Birch Lodge in New Brunswick, Canada. *That had to be something,* Danny thought. *What he would give to be a fly on the wall listening to those two old timers. The stories they must have swapped with each other on one of the best Salmon Rivers in North America. Amazing!* Then there was Vivian, the unofficial Mayor of Maidstone. She was the keeper of the history for the town. She was a force to be reckoned with especially if you were from the city or New Jersey. If you thought your fecal matter had no odor, Vivian would send you packing with your tail between your legs. It would be an easy day on Main Street. There were a lot of nice cars and pretty young ladies to checkout, and he was getting paid. This is working out, Danny thought; yes, life is good.

Chapter 12

Danny made his way slowly down Main Street. He took his time having nowhere to go except the end of the street and then turn around and stroll back. It was early evening. The sun was getting low on the horizon and the shadows were starting to grow longer. The day was cooling off. The car show was in the process of wrapping up. There were still quite a few cars and people milling around trying for one last glimpse or a few minutes to exchange histories about the cars with each other. Then the portable radio announced something that was just impossible to believe.

"All units stand by for an armed robbery," the dispatcher began the call. "State Police are reporting a second robbery of the toll booths by the same vehicle and person. The vehicle was last seen this time east bound headed towards Springfield."

Danny stared at the radio. *Big balls*, he thought. *Just how much money could you get at a toll booth?* There was also the fact that whoever was doing these robberies was on video from who knows how many cameras. *The guy had to be desperate and stupid. How could he think of getting away with not one, but two robberies? He would have been better off writing a bunch of bad checks at a bank.*

About ten minutes later, there was a third broadcast. A Pittsfield unit had spotted the vehicle on South Street in their town. Units were now in pursuit north bound on South Street towards the center of Pittsfield.

It won't be long now, Danny thought. A van isn't going to be able to outrun a cruiser. Danny was zeroing in on the radio call, the most exciting thing that happened today. Maybe even for the past several weeks. *Too bad they're way up north. I can't get in on the fun,* thought Danny. More calls were relayed by dispatch indicating that this was a full-blown chase with several units from Pittsfield and state troopers converging on the area. The state police were all off to the east, which had been the last known direction of travel. Somehow the suspect got off the highway without being detected and made his way north.

"Vehicle is now south bound on Route 9 at a high rate of speed with several units in pursuit," dispatch announced.

"Oh shit," Danny said out loud as he sprinted towards his cruiser that was 200 yards away, and they are headed right for us. *They can be here in less than five minutes if they don't get him stopped. We have all these people on the street and this slow traffic. This could be a disaster.* Danny yelled to the reserve officers who didn't have cruisers to clear the street. He and the other units would be heading north to block the road to keep the chase coming through the center of town.

Dispatch kept updating the progress and location of the chase. No police vehicles were between the suspect and town. They had to get far above Main Street on Route 9. They needed to get this chase stopped before it endangered everyone at the car show.

Danny jumped in the cruiser. He and the other two units headed north up Route 9.

"Dispatch, Unit 2," Danny barked between deep breaths from the 200-yard sprint. "Contact Pittsfield and all towns involved and advise them of the car show. We have

50

pedestrians and congestion clogging Main Street. We will attempt a rolling road block north of town on Route 9. Maybe we can deploy the stop sticks and bring this to a halt."

"Roger," was the curt reply.

Danny got back on the radio and went direct to the other units. He told them that he and Gary Carlson would proceed up to the intersection of Route 9 and Lee Road. He instructed Unit 3 to hold about a 1/10th of a mile just south of Lee Road. Danny wanted him to be ready to deploy the stop sticks.

"Lights out on all vehicles until we can see the chase coming down Route 9," he announced. "When the chase comes into view, we will bring the two cruisers at Lee Road out. We will then slowly head south blocking the suspect in and tying up the road. Unit 3 will standby with the stop-sticks. Hopefully between the chase vehicles behind and the three now in front, we can bring this chase to an end."

"Standby with the stop-sticks just in case he gets by us."

The plan sucked, thought Danny, but they didn't have time for much more. They were out of units to respond.

Everyone could hear the chase before they could see it. Pittsfield got on the radio call about the rolling road block. They were prepared to block the vehicle in on the sides and rear. The Maidstone Officers could hear what sounded like a dozen different sirens coming down Route 9, some, sounded very far away. Headlights came into view in the dusk of the evening with flashing blue and red strobe lights making a halo behind the van.

"Let's do it," Danny announced. He pulled his cruiser out and activated the lights. Both cruisers were in the roadway in a bladed position with the rear of the vehicles pointing towards the direction the chase was coming from.

They slowly made their way south watching for a reaction from the van.

"Perfect," shouted Danny. He watched over his shoulder as the headlights on the van dipped down abruptly, indicating that the driver had slammed on his brakes when he saw the cruisers up ahead. They were starting to get the chase under control. Things were slowing down. Now all they had to do was get the guy stopped. Maybe, just maybe, the guy would give up now that he saw he was boxed in.

A Pittsfield unit moved up behind the van and one came around on the driver's side of the vehicle. The rolling road block was starting to close in on the van. Things were slowing down. With all the flashing lights it looked like cruisers were everywhere. Hopefully the guy will come to his senses and just pull over. So far there have not been any radio broadcasts of shots fired or anyone being hurt. These were all pluses to this ending safely and right now. They just needed to contain him.

And then, everything turned to shit in a heartbeat. As the Pittsfield unit pulled up next to the van and began to crowd him over, the van rammed the police cruiser sending it into a spin. The cruiser went off the road into a row of hedges. Dust, dirt, grass, and small trees went flying. The flashing lights were lost in a cloud of debris. The lights behind the van were no longer visible. Danny tried to figure out where to place the cruiser to contain the van behind them, he couldn't even see the headlights anymore. A second later Danny watched a cluster of flashing lights behind him going in crazy directions. Through the dust and the low light conditions, he couldn't make out what was happening. And worse, he couldn't see the van.

"Shit;" he yelled "he got by us, but how?"

Danny kept craning his neck looking over both shoulders trying to figure out what had happened when the radio came back on with a now very excited Dispatcher informing all units that the suspect had rammed a Pittsfield Sergeant off the road. The chase was now north bound on Route 9, not south bound.

Relief and panic hit Danny at the same time. Relief that the chase was not headed for the center of town and the car show. Now panic that the chase was still on and getting more dangerous. Two armed robberies, a high speed chase, and then the ramming of the Sergeant. *I hope he's not hurt*, thought Danny as he maneuvered his cruiser in a 180 degree turn and headed north. With everyone trying to turn around, Danny was now the second vehicle behind a Lenox unit that was the closest to the van. Even though he was number two, he was still way behind. The van was pulling away. Danny floored the gas trying to catch up. In the distance Danny saw the lights take a left turn off Route 9 into a residential neighborhood. It was then that Danny realized that they were over the town line. He had no clue where that road went. The street was a big circle loop that crossed back over itself making a four-way intersection a short distance off Route 9. You could exit Route 9 in two places not that far apart to enter the loop, Danny didn't know that.

He made the turn and stopped in the middle of the 4-way intersection.

Which way did they go? Danny got on the radio to dispatch.

"Unit 2," Danny called. "I've lost them," he radioed. "We are on a side street off Route 9 north of the town line. I don't know the name of the street. Contact Pittsfield and find out where they are."

"Roger," was the short reply.

Then Gary Carlson pulled in and stopped behind Danny.

Danny exited the vehicle, thinking that he might be able to hear the sirens or see the flashing lights in the sky and figure out which way they went. He had no way of knowing they were headed right for him, he had only seconds to get ready. As Danny stood there with one leg still in the cruiser, the radio came on again, this time more frantic then the last. Danny figured they were going to tell him which way to turn so he started to get back in to the cruiser, that wasn't what he heard.

"All units," the dispatcher sounded out of breath," the suspect van has just rammed a second unit off a cliff."

"Oh shit," said Danny; not knowing which way to turn.

At that point he saw lights coming towards him down the street directly in front of him. Danny and Gary had their strobe lights on. Danny was in the middle of the intersection under a street light. All he could see were the headlights. The glare of the lights masked the vehicle behind them. He couldn't tell if it was a car or a van. If it was a van, was it the right van? Danny exited the vehicle pulling the shotgun with him. He moved just forward to get a clearer view, so that the strobe lights wouldn't be flashing in his eyes. *This has to be the van*. With the two cruisers in the intersection, it should stop. Danny still wasn't sure if this was the right vehicle.

Danny stepped forward and to the side as he held his left hand up with the right hand balancing the shotgun on his hip. The vehicle was still several hundred yards away. It was moving fast, faster than anyone would ever drive this street. The driver was not reacting to the flashing lights directly in front of him.

This has to be the guy, thought Danny. He lifted the shotgun to his shoulder and took a good Marine Corps off-hand firing position. He had no intention at this point of firing. The suspect should get the picture that stopping was an excellent idea. Danny still wasn't 100% sure this was the vehicle. He had a one or two percent of doubt, that disappeared when he heard the vehicle hit passing gear as the suspect jammed down the accelerator pedal and aimed right for him.

"Son of a bitch," yelled Danny as he pulled the trigger. Nothing happened. *Of all the dumb boot camp stunts*, Danny had forgotten to take the weapon off safe. "Idiot, idiot, you dumb shit idiot," cursed Danny.

He quickly pushed the off safety and took off running to get out of the way of the speeding van. Danny kept running, pulling the trigger and pumping the action to reload. Nothing was happening. Everything was in slow motion. He had covered maybe 20 yards in just a few seconds. He had pulled the trigger, he thought three times, but there was nothing. No boom, no recoil, no shell casings flying and no indication of impacts on the van.

The suspect made a screaming right turn just missing Danny by a few inches and speeding away, still on the same road that was going to lead him back to Danny.

Gary Carlson hadn't dismounted. He took off behind the van, as the suspect was pulling away. Danny was shaking. This was almost as bad as the Marines. In a way it was worse because he wasn't expecting this in Maidstone. Danny could not believe that the weapon had misfired three or four times. He couldn't remember how many times he had pulled the trigger as he ran backwards trying to get out of the way of the van. Then as he made his way back to the driver's side of the cruiser, he saw a path of four fired shotgun shells on the ground with smoke wafting up from the burst open ends.

Holy shit, I did fire. I must have missed. Four shots and the van kept going.

As Danny was trying to figure out what happened in the last 30 seconds, the radio barked again.

"All units, the suspect just tried to run over the officer that was run off the cliff." Danny listened as the second unit radioed in what had just happened to the suspect trying to run over Danny. Before the broadcast was finished, Danny saw the lights coming toward him again. He reached into his pocket, quickly loaded two shells and pumped the action.

Danny moved to the rear of the cruiser and took up a good firing stance.

He is going to stop this time, Danny told himself. Instead, Danny heard acceleration and not braking. Danny aimed high and centered on the windshield of the van. He waited until the last possible second giving the guy one last chance to stop.

The shotgun boomed; the stock recoiled into his shoulder. Danny knew this time he had fired and this time he didn't miss. The van went sailing past just inches away, and struck the curb 20 feet to his rear. The impact sent the van flipping end over end into a front yard of a nice up-scale residential home. Once again everything went into slow motion as Danny watched the vehicle cartwheel several times before coming to rest on the passenger's side. For a moment Danny stood there completely stunned by the events of the past few seconds. Regaining his composure, he ran to the van expecting to find the suspect, a dead bloody mess smeared across the windshield.

Danny stuck the barrel of the shotgun in the driver's side window and looked in. Nothing, no one, zip.

"Shit," Danny yelled and ran to the rear of the van where one of the two doors was open. Again, he stuck the shotgun inside. Once again there was no one there. Danny stepped back now, completely confused. He racked his brain trying to remember if he had any glimpse of the guy jumping out before the crash or if he had been ejected during the rollover. Danny kept the shotgun trained on the van. He was running out of ideas as to how this guy just disappeared.

Units from all over began arriving. A Pittsfield Detective was the first one there.

"Where's Tony," the Detective asked?

"Tony who?" countered Danny.

"The mutt driving the stolen van."

"You know him?"

The Detective ignored Danny and moved to the back of the van. "Tony, Tony, its Steve, Pittsfield Police Department, come out with your hands up."

Danny was about to tell him that no one was in the van when a muffled voice was heard from inside.

"Don't shoot! Please don't shoot. Tell the guy with the shotgun not to shoot. I'm coming out, don't shoot," was the response from the empty van.

To Danny's astonishment, the carpeting that had been on the floor that was now on the ceiling began to move. From underneath it emerged Tony moving under his own power. Slow, but moving; and he had his hands up.

Steve pulled him out the last few feet and cuffed him. The whole event was more than Danny could process. Everything happened in just a few minutes. Right now, his brain was on overload. Danny starred at the suspect, Tony. How did they know his name? How did he survive the crash? Danny looked the guy over. All he had were a few cuts on his face. No major lacerations, no broken bones, and almost no blood.

Chapter 13

Danny walked back to his cruiser and put the shotgun away. People from all over were responding to the scene. There were cruisers everywhere and an ambulance. Residents were coming out of their houses. Fire units were on the way, and volunteer firemen began arriving in their own cars and pickup trucks. Then there was this brilliant light.

Oh, damn, a TV news crew was now on scene. People were walking all over the crime scene picking things up. *This is turning into a real mess,* Danny was thinking. Then he saw a super squared-away looking State Police Sergeant walk into the sea of chaos. With all the jurisdictions involved and the fact that the armed robberies took place on state property, chances were that the State Police would take the scene.

Danny made his way to the State Police Sergeant. He was talking with a news videographer.

Danny was having a hard time speaking. He could only say a few words in a sentence, and then only after he thought about what he was going to say. He was so rattled he could not have a spontaneous conversation.

In a halting voice Danny asked, "Will the State Police be handling the crime scene?"

In a square shoulder posture, the State Police Sergeant turned to Danny and stated, "Yes, the State Police would be taking the scene and the arrest."

Danny was relieved as he had great respect for the State Police and their Major Case Squad. "Then I want you to know that I fired five rounds of double 00 buck," Danny said in a soft voice.

The State Police Sergeant pulled back on hearing the statement.

"Did anyone see you fire?" asked the Sergeant.

Danny, a little confused, replied, "I don't think so. It's dark, and this is a residential neighborhood. I don't think anyone was out."

"Hmm," was the reply. "Did anyone hear you shoot?" was the next question.

"Probably," said Danny. "It's a residential neighborhood. A shotgun makes a lot of noise."

Danny wasn't thinking very fast, still he knew he didn't like where this was going.

"Let's forget about the shotgun," the State Police Sergeant said, and began to turn away.

Danny was floored, unfortunately the words wouldn't come. Then he watched as the State Police Sergeant began squaring away his uniform, tucking his shirt in neatly, straightening his tie, and making sure his campaign cover was on right and tilted at a rakish angle.

Danny wondered what the hell is going on. With that last thought, the videographer switched on the lights and announced, "OK, let's do this." The State Police Sergeant took Tony by the arm and led him towards the camera. The "*perp*" walk began.

Stunned, confused, scared and just a tad outraged that he was unable to speak. Danny stood there, mouth hanging open.

This is it, he thought, *I am going down for excessive use of force, Tony, tries to kill me, twice. He tried to run over the Lenox officer twice and whoever that sergeant was he rammed down on Route 9. Then there are the two armed robberies. This trooper shows up after it's all over, and his big concern is looking good for the camera. I shot. I admitted I shot. I shot in self-defense, and this guy is going to try and cover it up.* Danny looked closely at the van for the first time.

Oh, shit, I didn't miss. This van has dozens of hits.

On closer inspection, he could see that the double 00 buck had dented, just not penetrated the van. There were somewhere in the area of 60 or more impacts. As Danny looked on, an older gentleman with a badge and a gun in civilian clothes approached the van with a young teenager. The teenager began picking out the chunks of lead from the double 00 buck rounds that were imbedded in the sides of the van. Danny motioned for them to back away, the kid just kept on picking out the lead.

This is it, Danny thought, *I am done, finished. I will be lucky if they just fire me, and I don't get any jail time.* Then the strangest of strange happened. The videographer asked the State Police Sergeant what he was going to charge Tony with. The State Police Sergeant gave a kind of shrug, dismissing the question.

"No, look at the van Sarge," said the videographer. "There have are a shit load of holes in it. There's no way that you can overlook that. Hey, I listened to the scanner," he continued. "He rammed one unit, and then rammed a second one off a cliff. Tony then tried to run this officer over. He then went back to get the guy he rammed off the cliff. Now he's down here for a second pass at this guy. You have several counts of assault on an officer, reckless driving, and maybe even attempted murder. You have to charge him with something."

60

Danny stood in silence. Here's a long-haired news guy coming to his defense with a State Police Sergeant who is trying to cover up a deadly use of force. If the Sergeant doesn't do something, this will blow up as soon as they clear the scene. Of course, the cameraman was making total sense. The crazy thing was that it was the cameraman and not the State Police Sergeant who was taking the initiative.

This is so messed up, thought Danny. *I am so screwed.*

If only he could calm down and get his voice back and get in on the argument. Slowly it did, just not before the State Police Sergeant nodded his head in agreement with the cameraman. Danny breathed a sigh of relief. Then Danny thought, *where the hell's the gun? This was an armed robbery, so where's the gun?* He started into the van looking for the gun.

As Danny worked his way into the front of the van, the State Police Sergeant questioned, "What are you doing?"

"Looking for the gun," was Danny's reply.

The smirking State Police Sergeant stated, "There isn't any gun, he used a knife."

Danny came back out of the van now more confused than ever. "A knife, a god damn knife?" shouted Danny. "No one on the hotline mentioned that a knife was used—just that we had two armed robberies."

This is totally screwed up, Danny thought, as he walked back to his cruiser to let dispatch know it was all over. Now the paperwork had to be done. For the life of him, Danny could not figure out why the no-nonsense State Police Dispatcher who sounded so professional had left the detail out that the suspect had used a knife and not a gun. And the fact that everyone except Danny knew who the suspect was.

Why in the world hadn't any of that been broadcast? Wasn't any of that important? Didn't someone somewhere think that passing along this information was relevant?

61

An hour or more later, Danny got back to the station, still trying to understand the events of the past several hours. No matter how hard he tried, it just would not come together.

Chapter 14

As he walked into the station, he was totally drained, mentally and physically exhausted. All he wanted was water, lots of water. Before he could get to the cooler, one of the reserve officers stopped him.

"Boy, did you miss all the excitement," he told Danny.

Danny was once more speechless. In his mind the past few hours went racing by. He kept wondering what he could have possibly missed. Hadn't he been in the damn middle of everything tonight? What did he miss?

"You should have seen it," said the reserve officer. "Vivian was a terror tonight. Hell on wheels and ready to kick some serious ass."

Now Danny was completely lost like this was an episode from some science fiction movie or that he was on some kind of mind altering drugs. He was sure of one thing: *Vivian wasn't at the shooting*. At least he didn't think so. Now he was trying to remember if she'd been there. No, he would have remembered that.

Danny starred at the officer and with an *OK, what the hell happened*, look that got the reserve officer talking.

"When you went running for the cruiser, what did you say?" asked the reserve officer.

"No idea."

"You said, and I quote: '*Get everyone off the street. There's a high-speed chase coming this way. We need everyone off the street now.*'"

Danny thought for a second and did recall yelling something like that. "So, what does that have to do with Vivian?"

"Well," the reserve officer said, "Vivian usually gives orders. In this case, she was taking orders and started clearing the street. When people didn't listen to her or were moving too slow for her liking, up she comes with the cane and a bunch of four letter words. We did get the street cleared with Vivian's help. We thought she was going to have a heart attack. A few of the New York types wanted her arrested for threatening and assault. We talked everyone down. You should have let the pursuit come into town just to support Vivian's personal declaration of Marshall Law. It was beautiful. She was a terror yelling and swinging the cane around. Fortunately, she was moving slow, fast for her age. The people she was going after were much younger, though not very bright because a few challenged her. When she got within striking distance, they ran. It was awesome watching her take charge. She was kicking ass and not taking any names."

"I need a drink," Danny said, as even more insanity came into the night.

"Scotch?" The reserve officer asked.

"Water, please, cold water, and lots of it." It had been a long few hours. You learned to expect things like this in the Marines, in Iraq, and Afghanistan, not Maidstone, Massachusetts. This was supposed to be the beautiful, peaceful Berkshire Hills. He could picture Vivian doing an uneven trot down Main Street waving her cane and backing people down. It must have been a sight to behold.

64

As the days and weeks passed, Danny waited to be called to testify at Tony's trial. Weeks turned into months. He finally called the court to find out when the trial would be.

"No trial," was the response from the clerk at the District Attorney's Office.

Danny was stunned. "Were the charges dismissed?"

"Oh no, not at all, he had already been convicted on prior crimes and was awaiting sentencing when he went on his own little crime spree. There were several other robberies, a couple of burglaries, and at least one more stolen vehicle. That night he was trying to get enough money together to get out of town because he was due in court on Monday to be sentenced to eight years in prison. With that and the other charges, he was looking at an additional twenty years. Tony accepted ten more on top of the eight. So, he should do about ten to twelve, depending."

Danny was once more at a loss. He figured it would be a long trial. His actions would be questioned under a microscope. It was already over and done, and he didn't have to say a word. He was relieved, at the same time wondering if it was justice for all those intentional crimes. All the property Tony had damaged. All the people he endangered. Well, it was out of his hands and over and done with. He had feared what District Attorney Cohen was going to think of his actions. This was a serious case and would get his attention even if he didn't prosecute the case personally. Danny had no idea what the state police had presented to the court. He did submit his report. What the troopers wrote up was unknown to him. This is a strange way of doing business, he thought, very strange.

Chapter 15

Danny had completed all the courses he needed to get into
Bob Marshall plus a few others. Somehow, he just wasn't
ready to go. Forestry and land surveying were both good jobs
and the outside work he was looking for. They were not going
to be as interesting as playing cops and robbers. There weren't
that many robbers in Maidstone, still there was a lot of cop
work. The medical calls, accidents, people acting strangely,
and citizens just behaving badly all made for an interesting
occupation. This wasn't the South Bronx or even Pittsfield;
still Maidstone did have its moments. You could never tell
when one of those moments would happen. Days you
expected trouble, like a Friday or Saturday night, could turn
out to be nothing. A quiet Sunday afternoon could turn you
on your head.

Danny was out on one of the dirt back roads on a
beautiful Sunday afternoon looking for dumped stolen cars.
The sun was shining, and the skies were mainly clear. It was
just a nice Sunday afternoon to drive around town and get
paid. Most of the vehicles he located were not stolen just
insurance give ups for the money. What car thief would steal a
car and drive it into the middle of nowhere to dump it and in
some cases burn it? Then the thief would have to find a way to
get back home miles from a paved road. No, most of the time
it was all about the insurance and the person's lack of ability

to keep up with the payments. Maidstone was a great place to try and pull off this type of insurance scam. It had plenty of dirt roads to go down and make a car disappear. So, for Danny, stolen car hunting in the woods usually turned up something.

He just hoped he could catch one in the act. Now that would be awesome.

Before he could find a burned-out Acura three miles from a paved road, the radio directed him back to the center of town.

"Unit 2," announced the broadcast, "we have a male naked on Main Street, heading west past the Big Dog Grill."

Danny starred at the radio and picked up the mike. "Roger."

This is so 1970s, thought Danny. *Do people still streak in beautiful downtown Maidstone,* he wondered? *We don't even have a college with a fraternity to require streaking for entry. Must be some out-of-towners,* he thought. *No problem. By the time I get out of the woods and back to Main Street, this guy will be long gone. Case closed by exceptional means.*

"Unit 2 to Dispatch, is the subject running?" Danny queried.

"Negative."

"Hmm," Danny thought, *that is strange. I never heard of someone streaking at a walking pace. Still it was going to take him several minutes to get there. This guy must have an escape plan or a buddy with a getaway car somewhere.* Danny had several funny thoughts as to where the guy put his wallet and car keys. Then things went sideways as only they could in Maidstone.

"All units," came the dispatcher in a panicked voice. Danny could tell something had changed in the streaking incident. *What now,* he wondered.

"Respond to **One** Main Street, the Congregational Church. The subject has just entered the church, and there's a service going on."

For a second, Danny starred at the radio as he stepped on the gas. He made his way as fast as possible out of the woods headed towards Main Street.

Maidstone had its eccentrics and off-the-wall people. Walking naked down Main Street into the Congregational Church had just raised the bar beyond the normal Maidstone off-the-wall activities.

All three units arrived within seconds of each other. The scene at the front of the church was best described as a cluster. It looked like everyone who had been inside was now standing on the steps or lining the sidewalk. In the center of it all was the pastor, kneeling on a tall skinny naked guy. As Danny ran up, he saw the guy was truly and absolutely bare-assed. All he had on was long blonde hair. Danny and the other officers moved in and took over. One officer had a blanket and covered the naked guy as best he could. The subject was handcuffed behind his back. He offered no resistance. As they rolled him over, the naked guy looked up at the pastor. In a quiet solemn voice, he said, "It is OK, Reverend; I forgive you for what you have done."

"You what?" shouted Danny, "You forgive him? You're the naked guy in church in the middle of a service. What the hell were you thinking?"

"This is my house, these are my people. I need to be with them on the day that they worship me," was the naked guy's calm and clear statement.

Everyone just stared trying to comprehend what this guy had just said.

"Come on," said one of the officers, "let's get him in a cruiser and get him outta here. This has been enough of a show for one day." The three officers lifted Mr. Naked to his feet and began to direct him to the nearest cruiser, Danny's. Now he began to resist though not in a fighting way. He just tried to turn and walk back up the sidewalk to the steps of the Church.

"No, no, this way," said Danny as he steered him towards the cruiser. "They have seen enough of you for one day. They need to get back to their service."

"This is my service. I need to be here for them. I need to show them the way. I should not be taken away from my home and service. It is not fair to the congregation."

The three officers stopped and looked Mr. Naked up and down. "Just who are you?" Danny asked.

In a soft, humble yet confident voice Mr. Naked replied, "Why God, of course."

Danny couldn't tell if he were serious, kidding, on drugs or maybe just plain nuts. He looked and sounded like he meant every word. He didn't appear to be on any drugs, which would have explained a lot of things. It wasn't a joke.

"Come with us," Danny directed. "We need to chat and clear up a few things. Once we get this straightened out we might be able to bring you back."

This seemed to appease the naked man who now had a wool Army surplus blanket draped over him. Danny looked at him more closely. *Oh shit,* he thought—*the blanket, the bare feet, long unkempt hair. With a little imagination, he did resemble one very famous person, and this was his day.* For a fleeting second Danny wondered if in fact he just arrested God. *Well, if this does turn out to be God, I better be nice to him. I may need his help in the future. A good reference from him could go a long way,* thought Danny.

The Pastor pulled on Danny's arm and in a not so pastorally way he stated that Mr. Naked was not welcome in the church.

Danny nodded and whispered back, "Just trying to keep him calm and get him outta here with as little fuss as possible. I suspect he will not be going anywhere for a while."

The Pastor nodded his approval. One officer stayed behind to get statements and write up a report.

Sunday in Maidstone—ya gotta love it.

Chapter 16

The ride back to the station was quiet. Mr. Naked/"God" sat in the back seat behind the cage looking out the window surveying the world outside the cruiser. He gave the impression of a dignitary observing the huddled masses as he, the Lord, passed by.

Danny moved "God" down into the cell block and began processing him. Mr. Naked continued to insist that he was "God" and in no way did he resist. A photograph and fingerprints were taken. "God" insisted that they would soon disappear as no one could capture his image. He seemed very confident and sure of himself. However, the computer showed that there were in fact loops, whirls, ridges and arches of a typical fingerprint. Through modern technology, they were able to get a picture of him, which he assured them was only temporary.

The officer who stayed behind for statements arrived back at the station and they now had a name, other than "God" for Mr. Naked. After everything that had happened, finding out that they had Thomas John Webb in the lockup was a real let down. Thomas John, aka TJ, still insisted that he was "God." He had never heard of a Thomas John Webb. They also knew where he lived. He had a small apartment behind the wine and cheese shop just off Main Street almost behind the police station. There was a girlfriend according to some people who knew him.

Who knew "God" would have a girlfriend, thought Danny. That thought quickly passed. In its place came a new concern. *Where is she, and is she all right?*

"We need to check out the apartment," Danny stated.

"We don't have a warrant," countered Gary Carlson.

Danny was heading for the door with no hesitation.

"We have a guy saying he's "God" in the lockup after walking down Main Street naked and into the Congregational Church. We now know there is a girlfriend somewhere. We don't know her condition. Let's at least knock on the door and see if she's all right. Seeing that TJ had no clothes when he got to the church, chances are the door isn't locked. Like where would he put the key? I would go on exigent circumstances to allow us entry."

"Whoa, that college stuff is making you some kind of attorney," said Carlson. Still he did follow Danny out the door.

They found the apartment, the door was unlocked. It was not what you would expect for someone who thought he was "God." It looked like a 15-year-old's room that mom forgot to clean for a couple of months. Sheets were tacked up over the windows. Food cans were all over the place. Some were moldy with half eaten contents. Books, newspapers, magazines and just plain junk were scattered everywhere. There was no evidence of a female having been there. They could not find any female products in the bathroom or female clothing in the closets. Nothing had a feminine touch. There was one interesting item. They found an Air Force identification card with the name Thomas John Webb. It had a photo of a cleaned up squared away Airman. If they didn't have the background, it would have been hard to match the

72

photo ID to the man calling himself "God" in the lockup. The hair was the first thing, there was also the large weight loss you could see in his face since the ID photo was taken. "God" had boney features and prominent cheeks and nose. The ID card photo showed a heathy and well fed young man with clear eyes and a hint of a smile. The hair was long for a Marine, though not for an Air Force type. It was clean and neatly trimmed. Of course, there wasn't a scraggly beard.

Well," God" had a second name now for sure. At least we have somewhere to start, thought Danny. They found some rambling and disjointed writings. Most had no conclusion or closing statement. They just stopped.

This guy has taken a long ride down to get to this point, thought Danny.

When they got back to the station, they found that nothing had changed. TJ still claimed that he was the savior. Information came in from the scene indicated that TJ/God had entered the church wearing nothing but a smile. He did however have a clock in his hand. It was one of those Baby Ben wind up clocks that you would find in a drug store.

"Let's start with the clock and get him talking. Maybe that will jog his memory," said Danny.

TJ sat quietly in the cell watching what was going on, making no comment.

"What was with the clock?" asked Danny.

"It was time," was the only reply.

"Time for what?"

"It was time for me to dwell in the House of the Lord. I am the "Lord God" and that is my house. That is where I should dwell," was the earnest response.

With a somewhat dumb look on his face as well as surprise, Danny blurted out, "you had an apartment, why move now?"

73

"Have you seen the apartment?" TJ asked. "How could I live in a place like that when there is this beautiful place of worship just a short walk away? It's my house anyway, so why shouldn't I dwell there? Plus, if I am there in the house of the Lord, then it will be easier for my followers to find me and speak with me."

In a strange way it was making sense to Danny, at least on the surface. TJ was being consistent. Danny thought back on the apartment; and given the option of living there or in the Congregational Church, he too would go with the church.

"Why did you go down Main Street and into the church naked? What was the purpose of that?"

"My people need to know it is me and see me for who I am. They need to see the real me, so they know that I am their Lord. They should know that I come in peace without all the trappings of some fake idol. That way they would know it was me and would have trust in me."

"Well, you scared the heck out of them. The minister wasn't too thrilled with your entrance. There were small children and older people in there. You should have thought of that before you went walking in that way. You should've done something to prepare them. Just dropping in naked and unannounced like you did wasn't very cool. You do know you made a bunch of people very nervous?"

TJ though about what Danny had just said. He frowned, his forehead furrowed, and his eyes narrowed, he was thinking about what Danny had said.

"Perhaps you're right. I assumed that once they saw me and heard my message they would completely understand what I was doing. I also didn't have a chance to explain anything when I was attacked and thrown out of my own house in front of my followers. Now that was not right."

For a moment Danny had to concede the point then remembered that as far as anyone knew this guy was not the Lord and Savior. TJ was convinced that he was and it didn't appear to be an act. Nothing was found in the apartment that would indicate drugs or alcohol. There were no track marks or crazy eyes, just one unkempt naked messiah.

Danny sat there wondering what to do with this guy. The Minister wanted to press charges along with half the congregation. There was a criminal, though minor at best, aspect to the day's events. They had taken him into custody, placed handcuffs on him, and transported him to the station. In legal terms he had been arrested, and they couldn't un-arrest him. *Well, we'll get him a jumpsuit and something to eat. That might help things along. However unlikely; maybe a night in the lockup will help clear his head. Where the hell is the Lieutenant?*

Danny asked one of the officers to hit the flush button for the cell so that clean, fresh water would be in the bowl. The water in there now could be a week old and TJ could not control the flushing as the button was in another room. This was to prevent a prisoner from flushing away evidence or flooding the cell block. Danny continued on with his questioning only to be interrupted by the sound of the toilet flushing.

TJ turned and watched the water disappear and new, fresh water flow in. Without hesitation he turned to Danny and stated,

"See, I wanted to flush the toilet, and all I had to do was think about it."

Danny shrugged his shoulders, stood up resigned to the fact that this wasn't going to wear off. Professional help would be needed. He wondered how many other people had arrested "God" on a Sunday. He then thought back to an Easter Sunday many years ago when Jesus had been arrested.

75

It didn't end well. *Oh, I am so screwed*, Danny thought, *so screwed. People who had arrested "Jesus" in the past were not well thought of.* Danny's mind wandered a little further. He pictured himself one day in the future in front of the Pearly Gates. Saint Peter was behind a very large desk with a huge book of names. He was going through it trying to find the entry for Danny. When he did, it wasn't good news. Saint Peter's eyes narrowed. He looked over his half glasses down at Danny with a very disapproving stare.

"Danny Gilcrest from Maidstone, we've been waiting for you."

He then pointed to a room for Danny to go in and wait. Someone wanted to see him. In his day dream Danny stepped into the room, and there in a chair was the Reverend from the Church. The Reverend looked up; and when he saw Danny he said, "Son, we are in big trouble."

Danny sat down next to him. Looking around the room Danny noticed two guys in togas sitting on the opposite side of the room.

"Who are those guys?" Danny asked.

"One is from Gethsemane, and his name is Judas. The other guy keeps getting up and washing his hands. He's Pontius Pilate. They have been here a while. Before Saint Peter did anything, he wanted the four of us here to take care of everything all at once. The big guy's schedule was tight. He didn't want to have to do things twice if he didn't have to. The other two have been here for a few thousand years. What's a few thousand years when you're talking about eternity?"

Yes, this could turn out really bad, thought Danny, *really bad.*

Chapter 17

The next morning nothing had changed. TJ still insisted that he was "God" and that if released, he was going to dwell in the house of the Lord. That would be his house, the really big white house, the one with the cross and a clean bathroom. No one had come forward to post the $250 bond. TJ had not made any phone calls. It was off to court. Danny got volunteered to be the escort. "You catch em, you clean em," the Sergeant said; and off to Berkshire Court in Great Barrington they went.

Fortunately, TJ was in a nice, clean orange jumpsuit, and he wasn't trying to take it off. When they got to court, TJ was placed in the holding area with the other prisoners. Danny went up with the paperwork for the Assistant District Attorney. After he finished explaining the events of the past 24 hours, the Assistant District Attorney looked at him and asked, "Is he still high?"

"No," Danny said, "there doesn't appear to be any drugs involved. This guy's girlfriend left him. He just turned himself inside out and stayed in his apartment for close to a month reading the bible and writing things down. When he came out, he was God."

"Well, what do you want to do?" asked the district attorney.

"He's an Air Force veteran, and I think the best place for him right now would be the VA psych ward. If I had the money, I would pick someplace else. Unfortunately, this guy is broke and doesn't have many options."

The District Attorney was relieved. It sounded like a plan. Now all they had to do was get the Public Defender to go along. That sounded easy until the Public Defender showed up—a screaming liberal who hated cops. He knew every arrest was a false arrest based on trumped up charges. In every case excessive use of force was present.

Danny went down to the lockup and picked up TJ who had been trying to get the other prisoners to see the light. They were not as understanding as Danny. Things had gotten heated. Fortunately for TJ, Danny showed up before things got physical. Danny knew that TJ was a few bricks short of a load. Still Danny liked him and wouldn't want anyone hurting him. Plus, on the off chance that he was really and truly "God," he wanted to be on his good side, just in case. Hanging out with Judas and Pontius Pilate for eternity was not something Danny was looking forward to. They entered the Public Defender's office, he glared at Danny. In a voice filled with contempt, he instructed Danny to wait outside. Danny hesitated and that triggered a demand to remove himself.

Danny still didn't move, and in a quiet voice said, "It might be a good idea if I stayed." The Public Defender started spewing the *US Constitution*, the Bill of Rights, attorney-client privilege and was about to continue when Danny stopped him.

"Look, counselor, how about you ask the very preliminary questions like name, home address, date of birth, where he works, you know the basic questions that he's already answered. If at the end you want me to step outside, I will."

The Public Defender was not too thrilled with being told what to do by this gestapo storm trooper with a badge, still he relented. "The minute I tell you to get out, you better be moving."

Danny nodded his head and gave him thumbs up and a quick, "Nooo problem."

Danny moved TJ to a chair and sat beside him opposite the Public Defender, who was behind his desk.

Danny turned to TJ and said, "Now tell him everything that happened when he asks. Don't leave anything out."

The Public Defender glared at Danny, despising the fact that he, a police officer, was advising his client what to do. Danny, not waiting for the Public Defender, directed TJ, "Tell him your name and where you just moved to and why."

The Public Defender was about to pounce when TJ announced, "I am your savior, the Lord God and I just moved into my house. This is the house of the Lord because that is where God should dwell. I was told that the Minister of the church was the one who threw me down the steps. I will deal with him later."

The Public Defender just stared open mouthed, not saying a word.

"Tell him what you were wearing and why," Danny prompted.

"Of course," said TJ. He went on to explain the events of Sunday.

While TJ was going into specific detail, Danny cut in. "Counselor would you like me to leave and get a coffee? I can give you some alone time."

The shaking of the head from side to side was all that the Public Defender could muster.

After all the details were relayed, the Public Defender only had one question, "How are you going to plead, guilty or not guilty?"

"Not guilty, of course" said TJ. "After all it's my house, and I make the rules."

With a deep sigh, the Public Defender stood up, "All rightie then, not guilty it is."

Oh no, thought Danny. He directed his questions and thoughts to the Public Defender who now was in more of a listening mood than when the interview started. "If he pleads not guilty and doesn't have a job or a means of support or a dime to his name, he's going into the correctional system for at least two weeks."

"Nothing I can do," countered the Public Defender, "it's his choice to plead not guilty. I can't make him change his plea." The Public Defender gestured towards the door, and stated that he more interviews to do before the court session started, and motioned toward the door.

Danny led TJ down to the food cart and bought him a coffee and a donut. They then went back into the court house. Instead of bringing TJ back down to the lockup to wait for his turn in court; Danny brought him into the court room. There he sat him down in the jury box. This was just an arraignment so there wouldn't be any jurors coming in.

The room began to fill up. The bailiff announced the arrival of the Judge. Everyone stood—everyone except TJ. The Judge looked over at the prisoner in an orange jumpsuit and the police officer. A scowl came across the Judge's face.

Danny turned to TJ. "Come on, you have to stand up."

TJ looked incredulous. "I am God; I stand for no one."

"Please," begged Danny, "do it for me, or I'm going to be in big trouble. You don't want that to happen, do you?"

"I guess not," TJ said as he slowly rose to his feet. "I guess he doesn't know who I am."

"You're probably right about that," said Danny, "I would suspect that he will find out soon enough."

As the cases were presented, the Judge kept glancing at Danny and TJ. Danny could tell that the Judge was trying to figure out what was going on and was distracted from the other cases. He just agreed with whatever was proposed by the District Attorney and whoever was for the defense. And then Thomas John Webb's name was called. Danny stood up, not TJ. He did not hear "his" name called.

Oh shit, here we go, thought Danny. "Come on, we have to stand in front of the Judge."

"Why?" asked TJ.

"Because we just have to—come on."

TJ slowly came to his feet and moved with Danny to the front of the court room. All eyes were on them. The court room seemed even quieter at that moment.

The Public Defender moved next to TJ. The court officer read the charges.

"Breach of the peace and criminal trespass," the court officer stated. This was followed by the brief description that TJ had walked down Main Street naked and into the Congregational Church while a service was going on. There was no mention of the fact that he believed he was the Lord. There isn't a criminal charge for that, so it wasn't relevant to the proceedings.

The Judge lowered his gaze at the defendant looking over his glasses with a look of disgust and contempt.

"How does the defendant plead?" demanded the Judge.

"Not guilty," stated the Public Defender.

"Bail?" the Judge asked the District Attorney.

"Your Honor, the defendant is being held on a $250 bond at this time. He doesn't have the funds to post that bail," replied the District Attorney.

"Bail is increased to $2,500," announced the Judge. It was plain he didn't like naked men walking the streets of Maidstone or interrupting a church service. "Next case," he called.

Danny looked at the Public Defender who was about to walk off.

"Hey, aren't you going to do something, say something?" Danny demanded of the Public Defender?

"Excuse me," said the Judge.

The Public Defender did not respond.

Everyone was staring at Danny, especially the Judge.

"My apologies, Your Honor, at the next recess, if I could have a word with you I think there is some information you need to hear." Danny could not believe that the Public Defender had not spoken up. Now he had to carry the ball for the guy he arrested.

The Judge looked at the people standing in front of him trying to decide whose life he was going to make miserable first.

"Recess, now!" and the Judge banged down his gavel. Before the "all rise" could be announced, he was out the door and into his chambers followed by the District Attorney, the Public Defender, Danny and a very dignified and confident TJ.

"This better be good," shouted the Judge as he dropped into his chair not offering anyone a seat.

"Could the court officer wait with the defendant outside for a few moments?" asked Danny.

The Judge waved his hand at the court officer, and TJ marched out of the room.

Danny knew he had to get this right for TJs sake and for his own, or he would never forgive himself. Danny knew that he was Thomas John Webb and not God. He still had to do something.

"Your Honor, he thinks he's "God," Danny began. As quick as he could, he laid out what had happened on Sunday.

The Judge listened intently. "You're sure there are no drugs involved?" he asked.

"None that we could find and no criminal history of any kind," said Danny.

"You think the VA is his best option?" queried the Judge.

"Not knowing the system all that well, I think that would be better for him and the community," said Danny. "He isn't a criminal—just sick and needs help. The VA has a secure facility where he can get treatment. If we lock him up in jail, he won't get the help. If he makes bail, then he's out on the streets and could decide to go back to church. The nasty mutts in jail will eat him alive. He is a veteran, he served, and now he needs help."

The Judge directed that the suspect be brought back in.

"Well, son, what's your name?" asked the Judge.

The ambulance arrived about 20 minutes later.

Chapter 18

Danny was feeling pretty good about himself. He had gotten a fellow vet the help he needed and kept him out of jail. The Judge who was never known as a happy guy was not red in the face with him, so he put that on the plus side. Then on Tuesday came the phone call. Danny was about to pour a cup of coffee when he was suddenly interrupted.

The Dispatcher called out to Danny in the break room. "What did you do now?"

Danny looked at the coffee pot he hadn't even touched, wondering how he had screwed up the coffee. He took a step back trying to figure out how walking up to the coffee pot had triggered something. Before he could continue his self-analysis, the Dispatcher added, "The Supervising District Attorney is on the line, and he wants to speak to you."

Danny hesitated for a second then asked, "Is it Marvin Cohen?"

"Yes," came the reply, "and he doesn't sound happy."

"No problem," countered Danny. "He is one of my professors, and he never sounds happy. It probably has something to do with a course I am taking."

"I don't think so, pick up on Line 3."

"Officer Gilcrest, how can I help you?" was the military response to answering a phone.

The voice on the other end was not happy. It was not a call about his studies. In classic Marvin Cohen, it was a long drawn out, over officious with just a hint of arrogant tone. How could anyone know he was being nice?

"Well, if it isn't the one-man judicial system for Berkshire County," came the first greeting. "I am so very glad that you have time in your busy and full schedule to accept my call."

Oh, shit, was the first thought that crossed Danny's mind. *Think; this has nothing to do with school. I am about to incur the wrath of the most senior law enforcement official in Berkshire County and I have no clue why. What could I have possibly done?* Before he came up with an idea, District Attorney Cohen continued on.

"I see you've had a busy weekend."

Oh, shit, Danny said to himself; *it's about arresting God. What did I do to screw that up? Maybe he hurt someone. Maybe he committed suicide. Oh, shit.*

"Let me see if I have the facts straight," said Supervising District Attorney Cohen in an even more abrasive and condescending tone. He was known for his brutal treatment of those who crossed the judicial system and him personally. Officers who engaged in excessive use of force or skirted the law would know his displeasure in spades. It wasn't that an officer couldn't use reasonable force. Cohen had no problem with that. It was when every arrest an officer made resulted in the arrestee being brought to the emergency room prior to booking. That could get you in the cross hairs. Danny hadn't hurt anyone this weekend. He had arrested God. Maybe that was worse.

"So, you responded to a disturbance, investigated the incident, made the arrest, booked the prisoner, transported him to court, and then took over the prosecution AND the

85

defense of the suspect in open court. Am I right so far?" Supervising District Attorney Cohen asked.

Danny was trying to think as fast as Attorney Cohen was speaking. It was no small feat trying to hear the facts and tone out the abrasive sarcasm.

"I guess that's about right."

"Oh, oh, oh, I forgot the best part. You then took over for the Judge and had him reverse his decision. Now do I have it right?" Cohen asked.

"I just made some suggestions," Danny blurted out.

"Is there some reason that you didn't feel it would be appropriate to include the District Attorney assigned to the case when you came up with these, suggestions? And pray tell; when did you start working for the Public Defender's Office?"

Danny was back peddling and going on the defensive. It was apparent that the Supervising District Attorney was not pleased with his performance of the past two days. Wait a minute.

"No, Sir," said Danny, the determination and conviction of a Marine coming back. "That guy is a veteran, he is sick and needed help, not a jail cell. No one was asking the right questions. Then because he is sick, he didn't know what to say to help himself. I suspect that today and for some days or weeks to come, he will still think he's God. That line of thinking won't help him in jail."

"So, you are saying that my District Attorney screwed up?"

Danny was back in the game. He should have been intimidated by this man and his position. He knew he had done the right thing. He would stick to his guns.

"Not at all, Sir, the District Attorney was following the law and where it took him. I was just thinking way out of the box. I know veterans who have had their share of problems and need help. I have never heard of one who believed he was God. I think that when all the facts came out, everyone figured that sending him to jail was wrong. Now getting him into the VA psychiatric ward was the best course of action given the circumstances." Danny took a deep breath and waited for the next broadside he knew was coming. Cohen's response surprised him.

"Excellent," Came an almost shouted response from District Attorney Cohen. "Keep up the good work and keep thinking outside of the box. Now next time please include the rest of us in the judicial system, or we are all going to be out of a job. We are all here to do the right thing, just remember us the next time." And the line went dead.

Danny stared at the now humming phone.

The Dispatcher who had heard one side of the conversation asked, "Well?"

Danny slowly placed the phone back in the cradle still trying to digest what had just happened.

"I think I just got an ass chewing from the Supervising District Attorney that was followed by an atta-boy."

"Did he say, *I will have your ass,*' questioned the Dispatcher?

His brain was a little confused at this point. He thought back trying to remember the exact words. "No, he never said that," Danny stated after several moments of deep thought.

"Then you're fine. Everyone who the Supervising District Attorney ever went after always had the warning that, '*I will have your ass.*' If he didn't say it, you're golden. If he did say it, then you're toast."

Danny kept thinking long and hard if those words were ever mentioned. He racked his brain. Fortunately, he could not recall that statement or one close to it. Time would tell.

The Dispatcher asked, "Why didn't you do an emergency commitment?"

"A what?"

"An emergency commitment, officers have the authority to take someone who is acting crazy down to the Emergency Room for a psych. evaluation by a doctor. That usually turns into an emergency commitment for at least 24 hours."

"I never heard about that."

"Didn't the Lieutenant tell you?"

"No."

Danny walked back to the coffee pot and called out, "Is the coffee safe?" The Dispatcher gave him a strange look and went back to the phones.

Danny would be in Supervising District Attorney Cohen class this week. Attorney Cohen loved to use real Berkshire County situations to explain bad behavior. Most people in class knew of the situations. They were aware of the people and officers involved so they could directly relate to those incidents. *Oh please,* thought Danny, *don't let me be one of his examples.*

That week Danny dreaded going to class not knowing if he was going to be the main subject of discussion. He sat in his chair pretending to be taking notes and trying to figure out what to say when the bomb was dropped.

The bomb was never dropped. Attorney Cohen never called on Danny. For the most part, he never even looked at him. Then as everyone was filing out of class, there was the dreaded call.

"Officer Gilcrest!" boomed the voice.

"Yes Sir," Danny said in a subdued voice just waiting for the verbal body slam.

"You have a nice weekend and try and stay out of trouble."

Danny was stunned and almost wished that Attorney Cohen had yelled at him and gotten it over with, but he didn't. So, Danny would have to wait for the next time. *I am glad he's on our side,* Danny thought. *Not necessarily my side, he was on the cops' side.* Danny began to review everything that had happened. The Supervising District Attorney for Berkshire County had taken a personal interest in this very minor, though interesting case. Why hadn't Lieutenant Lincoln Cornell gotten involved? Cornell was Danny's immediate supervisor and never said word one about the arrest or going to court. He should have known what to do. He had two days to step in and instead left it to Danny, a rookie. He never mentioned an emergency exam.

Now Danny had direct personal contact with Supervising District Attorney for Berkshire County Marvin Cohen. This would be the next step in getting closer to a blast from a shotgun. Life takes some long and strange roads. Most people are not aware of it until the end and Danny was no exception. Then again, how could he possibly make that connection? Up to this point, there was nothing to indicate any type of danger. For the moment there wasn't any. The connections had to be made. The associations developed. It was like a long, seemingly disjointed physics problem where everything had to line up. If it didn't, the outcome would be different. This time, everything was lining up. Just like the physics problem, until you got to the very absolute end, you had no idea what the outcome was going to be.

Chapter 19

School went on, life went on: accidents, medical calls, thefts, unusual behavior, and the occasional drunk kept things interesting. Small towns are not immune from everything no matter how nice they are. Friday nights were always interesting, something would happen. In a way, Danny looked forward to the challenging calls. He felt guilty because if they were challenging and interesting then someone had to get hurt or be a victim. Danny didn't want to wish that on anyone. He didn't want someone to get hurt so he could have an interesting night. His wishes had no bearing. He could wish or not wish all he wanted. It was up to other people to determine what would happen at any given moment. He had no control what-so-ever over those actions. All he could do was be prepared, respond and do the best he could.

In the big city departments, you might only spend a few years on the road as you worked your way up the promotional ladder. There were all the other jobs that needed to be done that for the most part were away from the road and didn't involve rotating shifts. You could be a school resource officer or be assigned to records or the training unit. You might get assigned to desk duty or as a community outreach group. You could rotate into one of the investigative units, or you might get promoted. In Maidstone you might be a patrolman your entire career and spend every shift on the road in a cruiser handling calls. That was just the way it was, and Danny knew it.

Third shift on a Friday night usually was hopping for the first three or four hours, then the town would go to sleep and nothing would happen. Once the bars closed and the shows ended, there was nothing going on. There would be almost no traffic as the town tucked in for the night. Drinking and drugs would fuel the problems. Drunk drivers, accidents, domestics, medical emergencies would peak in the hours around midnight. A half hour after last call, it was like someone turned a switch. Anything that was going to happen took place before 2 AM. This wasn't the Big Apple; this was not a city that didn't sleep. It did sleep and very soundly, most of the time.

Things were busy that late summer night. No one expected how bad September 11/12, 2009 would be. The town had several softball games going on. There was an exhibit at the Andrea Smythe Gallery. A concert was on at Tanglewood up the road in Lenox. Busy, but most would be home in bed or back to their inn or motel by midnight or at the latest 1 a.m. This was not a late-night party town. It was into partying, just not late night.

Shift change was almost a social time at the police station. Second shift would be coming off getting ready for a few beers and maybe a late night west coast ball game with the Sox, of course. Third shift would be coming on picking up where second shift left off. At roll call the new shift would be updated on how the evening was shaping up. Coffee would flow, and conversations would take place—briefings, B.O.L.O.s from other departments and any wanted people that might be in the area. The change would take anywhere from 15 minutes to a half hour, depending on what was going on and if units could come off the road from their calls.

Tonight's shift change would last for hours, more than the entire shift.

Both shifts were either in the station or just coming off the road. Reserve officers were present having been on extra duty or doing volunteer time. Just before 11 PM, the switch board lit up. Every 911 phone line and the routine lines seemed to come on all at once—not a good sign. Officers picked up their equipment and waited to hear the dispatcher's side of the conversation. Everyone knew it wasn't going to be good. When that many calls came in at the same time, it was not going to be an easy night.

In the first few seconds, officers started for the cruisers. Second shift, third shift and reserve officers grabbed their gear and headed for the door. The dispatcher was repeating what he was being told as he answered the various lines, and his confirmation was not good.

"Car vs pedestrian."

"Multiple Injuries."

"Possible fatal."

"Vehicle has evaded heading south on Route 9."

"Please send multiple ambulances."

As the calls were coming in, the officers were out the door. As the phone was answered and the dispatcher hung up, the line would flash again with another call reporting the accident. It only got worse as the details came in. This was going to be a challenging night, and not a good one. There would not be a good outcome for anyone. No one knew that as bad as this was at the moment, it was going to get worse. Or that Danny would be one step closer to a shotgun blast.

The run to the scene was actually quite short. The first unit arrived on scene in less than two minutes from the original call. The location was at an intersection with Route 9 and a small side street. There was a street light to one side that offered limited illumination. The entire accident scene spanned several hundred feet with a good portion not being on the road. It was grotesque. One very young person was lying just at the edge of Route 9 and showed no apparent signs of life. A second individual was found on the side street and was still alive, God only knows why. Her right leg was up over her right shoulder extending straight back past her head. She was still breathing and mumbling, just nothing that anyone could understand. There was a third individual about 200 feet off the road. The tire tracks led to him, and he wasn't moving. His upper body was smashed into a bloody pulp. They were all young, not more than in their mid-teens, and there was so little light that figuring things out was difficult. Units arrived one after the other. Officers moved from one body to the next, finally coming back to the young lady with her leg up over her shoulder. She was the only one showing any sign of life. Officers began by flashlight trying to determine how bad she was and what first aid to do. The injuries were beyond first aid and bandages. As they cut what clothes she had on, the damage came into view. It was a miracle that she was still alive. She was split almost in half from her tail bone to her naval. Her internal organs were completely exposed. Strangely, there was very little bleeding. She was still breathing, had a pulse, and was moaning. No one knew how could someone suffer so much damage and not be dead?

The ambulance arrived. Everyone looked at each other with the one question: *now what do we do*?

No one from the police, the fire department or the ambulance had ever seen an injury like this. Everyone just starred. Just how do you treat and transport someone in this condition?

Danny looked at the rag-doll-like body watching the chest continue to go up and down, sucking in air and life. Everyone looked on, and no one moved. Out of the three kids, she was still alive and had a chance. They had to do something.

Danny hesitated and then moved in.

"OK, this is a mess; we've got to get her to a trauma center if there is any chance of her making it. She isn't bleeding much. Let's pack the wound as best we can. Someone get the scoop stretcher and get her out of here and into an ER as fast as we can. I think we should leave the leg in place as moving it may cause too much pain, and she might start bleeding. Bottom line is we have to get her out of here and into a hospital. This is way beyond anything we can handle."

Danny's experience with IEDs helped. Looking at someone so young and so damaged still got to him. The paramedics from the ambulance were not hard-core Navy Corpsman that a Marine could yell for and then move out and leave the treatment to them. At a few minutes past 11 PM, in the small town of Maidstone, Massachusetts, this young lady's chances for survival depended on them. They were the only ones who could make it happen.

As gently as six people could, they packed her internal organs. With great care they put the scoop stretcher under her and clipped it together. Six people from the police, fire and ambulance carried her to the gurney and then into the ambulance. No one thought she would make it, still they were trying. They had to give it their best shot. They could not just give up. There were two dead already, if only they could save one of the three. Prayers and promises were made. It was all they had left. Then the ambulance departed. Radio calls were made for a helicopter to make its way to the hospital in Great

Barrington for transport to a trauma center once the young lady was stabilized.

Now drained, bloody, and sad, the officers turned their attention to the two bodies and the missing vehicle. There were the tire marks showing that the vehicle had left Route 9 and crossed over the intersection. The vehicle then drove onto the grass and into a small planted berm. The impact appeared to be in the intersection on the edge of the side street. Glass, shoes, and blood were spread out in this location. It appeared from the tracks in the grass that the vehicle had hit the berm and then backed up only to pull back onto Route 9 and continued on. The boy must have been on the hood as his body was dumped on top of the berm. The young lady on the way to the hospital was found back at the intersection with the second female victim.

Danny heard over his portable radio that one of the units was informing Dispatch to contact all surrounding towns to be on the lookout for a vehicle with heavy front-end damage. The vehicle was last seen heading south on Route 9 towards Great Barrington. Danny knew that every unit from the area towns would be on alert and looking for this vehicle. This was about as serious as it got in the Berkshires. This guy needed to be caught after what he had done.

Everyone was trying to sort out the scene when a car pulled up and the driver got out. He walked up to the first officer he saw and announced, "I got him."

"You got who?" asked the officer.

"The driver of the hit and run," was the response.

Everyone at the scene froze in position. All conversation stopped.

"How do you know it's the driver?" asked the officer.

"His car is disabled a half mile from here with the entire front end smashed in. His passenger is in the back seat curdled up in a ball crying. I came by here on my way home and found them on a side street just before I turned for my house. The kid is in shock and is just staring straight ahead. Did anyone die here?" he asked.

"Two, maybe three," was the short response as the officers converged on the car.

There was no resistance. No denials. No statements. Just a blank stare from the person identified as the driver. The passenger was pulled from the back seat and all he kept asking was, "Are they all right," and "Are they OK?" The two were about the same ages as the three they'd hit.

Wallets were removed from the two suspects. Danny recognized both names. He didn't know these two personally, but he did go to high school with someone from their families. He still didn't know the three in the intersection. The two still at the scene were not recognizable. He never got a clear look at the young lady they had transported. He was concentrating on the injuries and never looked at her face closely. He really didn't want to.

After getting the two boys out of the civilian car and into cruisers, one officer took off following the citizen who had located the vehicle. Moments later the officer came up on the radio informing all that this was indeed the evading vehicle. There was blood everywhere. The front end and windshield were smashed. Both mirrors were missing.

Danny looked back to the intersection, and there were two vehicle mirrors on the ground. One was just into Route 9 and the other lying on the side street. Well, we have the connection, thought Danny. A lot of good this is going to do the three kids who got hit.

The next broadcast was that the Regional Accident Reconstruction Team was being called out of which one of the officers was from Maidstone. Block the road. Detain any witnesses. Hold the suspect and his passenger and do not touch anything. It was only twenty minutes past eleven, and there was still a full shift ahead of them. It was going to be a long night. What Danny didn't know was just how long.

Thinking that their plate was full and nothing else was coming down, everyone turned to helping secure the scene and transport the prisoners back to the station. Suspects and the officers were drained. No one was talking, overwhelmed by the events of the past hour.

As they arrived at the station, they were informed that the female they had transported didn't make it. The one ray of hope was gone. The one chance for something good to happen and it just went down the shitter.

In a very unprofessional, totally emotional outburst, Danny turned to the driver, the 17-year old brother of one of Danny's high school classmates, and shouted, "What the hell were you doing? You just killed three people. What hell did you think you were doing?"

The kid was in tears and on the verge of throwing up.

"We were just racing with another car, we didn't mean it. We had passed the car we were chasing when here comes a car in the opposite direction. I swerved to the right to keep from hitting it head on. They were just there on the side of the road. I never saw them until I hit them. I'm sorry, so sorry," he sobbed.

Danny looked at the kid. He had just gotten a full confession. One he couldn't use. No Miranda, no attorney, under duress. *I screwed up* thought Danny, *I blew it*.

Danny got back to the station and dropped off the driver to be processed and then went back to the scene. He found the supervisor of the reconstruction team and related what the kid had told him and the fact that he had not been Mirandized, and how he had screwed up.

97

The Supervisor listened to him and then took him aside.

"Relax," he said. "We have all the physical evidence we need. A confession would be nice, we still have him. We won't use the confession, and we don't need it. After looking at the scene, I'm surprised he didn't get punched out. We got it from here. Go get a coffee and write up your report. Leave the confession out. Besides, his passenger is a mess and won't shut up. They were just out to do a little rat racing with friends. Then wham, the driver hits these three and sends one right into the passenger's side of the windshield. Here is this kid staring at the smashed face of another teenager staring back at him through the glass. When the car came to a stop, the kid slid off the hood and onto the ground. The passenger has been crying the entire time and has been throwing up. In between trips to the bathroom to clean up, he's been giving one of the officers a statement. It's over, the driver's toast. Like I said, we will take it from here. Go get cleaned up, you're a mess."

Danny walked away. He knew he screwed up. He was better than this. Things like this should not get to him, it had. Maybe the squirrels were coming out. Maybe his stress level was finally filling up. Maybe he should get a bunk with TJ/God for a few weeks.

If only the night ended this way. Evil does not take a day off or give you a break when you have a bad day. And the day wasn't over by a long shot.

Chapter 20

Not twenty minutes later, a call came in from the west side of town. Several individuals had been spotted entering cars in a residential area. They were observed going through the center consoles and glove boxes and grabbing whatever they could. The caller stayed on the phone giving real-time updates as to where they were. The person reporting the incident had even spotted where the getaway car was parked and what details he could see. Because both first and second shifts were still on, the response was impressive by Maidstone standards. Instead of the normal full response of two or three cars, six units were on their way. After the events of 11 p.m., none of the officers were in an understanding mood. The caller continued to relay information even as the first unit arrived. There were no lights or sirens to warn the suspects of the officers' approach. As the first unit arrived, the suspects froze until they realized that it was the police. Quickly, they made a mad dash for the getaway car parked on another street. Thanks to the caller, units were pulling up to that vehicle at the same time the officers were approaching the suspects. Not knowing what they had besides people breaking into cars, the officers came out with guns drawn, just in case. Every possible cop demand was shouted at the suspects who, seeing they were surrounded dropped to the ground and gave up. The three were cuffed, searched and then placed in three different police cruisers. A check of the getaway car found cell phones, chargers, CDs, sunglasses, change, flashlights, a laptop, a couple of tablets, and a small amount of marijuana and beer.

This wasn't the great train robbery; it was a good grab all the same. It was finally a positive note for one horrible evening. It wasn't going to make up for three deaths. Still the feeling of success, however small, was having a positive effect on all the negative of the evening.

A tow truck was called for the getaway car and the suspects were transported back to the station for processing. No questions were being asked. The lesson had been learned. No interrogation until all the paperwork had been done with the I's dotted and the T's crossed.

"Hey, did anyone run the plate on the car to see who owns it or if it was stolen?" Danny asked.

All the officers looked at one another. All that came up was a blank look and a few shoulder shrugs.

"I'll do some computer checking when we get inside and run these three for warrants and priors," announced Danny. They went in; the computer search would have to wait.

Chapter 21

As they walked by the control room door to the processing area, everyone stopped in mid-stride. The Dispatcher was on the phone standing up staring at the console like he could see through the phone to the person who was calling. No one could believe it when the Dispatcher shouted into the phone, "What do you mean, your wife is dead, you just shot her?"

Everyone heard the words, suspects and the officers. They heard it; they just didn't believe it. Then the Dispatcher repeated it again, this time louder. It was starting to sink in that this was for real and was as serious as it gets. The Dispatcher repeated it a third time still staring at the console trying to see what was going on at the house. If there had been any doubt before, it was gone now. The Dispatcher turned to the officers just outside the door. He still had the phone in a death grip in his right hand. His mouth hung open and his eyes gave a look of total disbelief. He was in shock. It took him a moment to put the words together. No one in Maidstone had ever had a call like this. Everyone remained motionless waiting unbelieving, still knowing what was coming. Someone had just shot their wife. Now all they needed was to find who and where. It was only a few seconds, but it seemed like a short life time before the Dispatcher could get it together.

In a slow, halting voice with each word separately spoken, he informed the officers that Bradford Worthington had just shot his wife at their home on Berkshire Trail Drive. In slow motion he hung up the now beeping phone and turned back to the console and sat down. He stared at the straight ahead in disbelief hoping that the words would be taken back, or that what he heard was wrong, and would soon be corrected. It didn't happen.

The officers began moving in all directions at the same time. Everyone was headed for the door grabbing their gear to get back in the cruisers. *The prisoners; now what?*

"Screw-em!" Danny grabbed the three, and they were pushed into one cell still handcuffed. He slammed the door and followed everyone out. "These three mutts can wait."

It was a mad dash to Berkshire Trail Drive. This time there was no stealth in the response. Every light and siren was activated. Even the Regional Accident Squad was responding. At almost the same instant the first two units arrived, followed seconds later by the other four.

It was dark, and there was a little light coming from the house and a street light down the road. This was a newer neighborhood with larger yards and lots of trees. Most of the houses were garrison colonials with three and four bedrooms and a two-car garage. These houses and lots were much bigger than most people in their mid-twenties could ever afford. This wasn't a Maidstone estate; it was way above someone just starting out in life.

The first thing that Danny heard was screaming. It was a male voice—not a female—screaming in pain and in anguish like a wounded animal. He drew his weapon and proceeded up the driveway towards the house. It was dark for the most part with deep shadows and dappling light in others. Danny was trying to get an understanding of the call and figure out

102

the threat. They made their way past what looked like a brand new black Cadillac Escalade in the driveway.

After the call, it took the Dispatcher a few seconds to compose himself and snap back into police mode. He tried to call back to the house for more details, there was no answer. He relayed that information to the responding units. Were they walking into a trap? Is someone really dead? There were too many unknowns, and no time to figure it out. Going forward was the only option, going forward into the unknown.

The screams were coming from the front yard. As Danny and the first officer got closer, they could see a male sitting on a stone wall next to the walkway. Dim light coming from the windows of the house put him in an eerie glow. His body glowed in the light. His screams had become less, but hadn't stopped. He was wearing only shorts and white athletic socks, no sneakers or shoes. He was bare chested, and that shiny glow was because he was covered in blood. He was rocking back and forth in obvious pain holding his left arm.

Danny was trying to make the connection between the call *I shot my wife* and this guy sitting here covered in blood and apparently injured. There had been no mention of a male being hurt. Was this the guy who made the call, or is there someone else?

Is there a suspect still around?

Who is this guy?

Where's the wife?

Is this the husband?

A voice came out nowhere and demanded, "What happened?" It was one of the police officers.

Then, between screams and sobs, they heard it again. "My wife is dead, I shot her," said the blood-covered man.

"Where is she?" came the next demand from out of the darkness.

"She's upstairs in the bedroom, she's dead. I killed her," was the reply through tears and moans.

Danny reached down and pried the right hand away from the left arm. He thought that there might be a weapon there. Now he found out where the blood was coming from. There was a chunk of his hand missing down to the bones. The skin was peeled back to the wrist. Danny's first reaction was, *That has got to hurt.* At the same time, *how the hell did that happen if he just shot his wife?* It didn't look like a suicide slash that he might have inflicted on himself.

They were getting some answers; still none of it was making sense.

Danny yelled for a first aid kit and an ambulance and then started into the house behind the first officer. They came in with guns drawn still not feeling they had the whole story. They made their way to the upstairs bedroom and found the wife. She was on the floor at the side of the bed. The lights were all on, and the scene was surreal. The young lady laid there with her eyes open and a blank surprised look on her face. The back-left side of her head was missing. It was no longer part of her and was plastered on the wall, the floor, and the bed. Part of her skull lay on the hardwood floor like a broken piece of grey/white pottery, and there was blood. There was a long strand of her brown hair sticking out of a hole in the wall. Her body was entangled in the sheet and blanket that was twisted around her body. She rested in a seating position with her back against the wall. Above her was a red smear of blood that marked her slide down. There was a ghostly red outline of the left side of her body made by the blood spray pattern from the explosion of the shotgun blast.

Underneath the sheet and blanket you could see that she was naked.

There was no doubt she was dead. A short-barreled shotgun lay on the floor a few feet away. Danny could see that it was a large bore slug gun for deer or bear. That size round would do serious damage to whatever it hit. Danny looked from the shotgun to the young lady and back. He stared at the lifeless body that did not look real. She looked like a poorly arranged mannequin that had been dressed up to look like a corpse. The face was not damaged, lifeless, but still intact. It was a face Danny had seen for at least four years, riding the bus with her every day of the school year. He remembered that at some point he had a crush on her as she was one of the prettiest girls in school, and way out of his league. Back then she had been dating the son of a very wealthy owner of one of the biggest trucking companies in Western Massachusetts. Danny could not compete with a guy who had money, a car, and access to a boat at age 16. Way back then he had heard that things were loud and difficult between the two. At times things had turned into violent physical confrontations. Even with that kind of track record, she had still married him, and now it had come to this. Danny had not even recognized Brad the darkness, the pained look, and all the blood had distorted his features contorted in anguish. Now with the name from the Dispatcher and the wife upstairs, Danny was able to see the face of Brad, a guy who had it made in his twenties, and a murderer who was going to prison.

"Come on, we need to clear the house. There might be someone else in here, or they might have kids," said Gary Carlson.

Oh shit, Danny thought, *I don't remember any kids.*

If this got any worse, they would be finding children, hopefully alive. With great hesitation, they made their way through the house. To their relief, they found no one else.

While the house was large and expensive, the two lived like teenagers. Dishes were stacked in the sink. Clothes were piled everywhere. There was no food in the refrigerator to speak of. One bedroom that was used for ironing looked like someone was getting ready for a big tag sale. Clothes were just left everywhere on the floor.

Crazy thoughts run through your mind at a time like this. Danny was thinking about the times he had seen the couple out in town. Every time they seemed to be dressed like they had just walked out of an upscale clothing ad. *They must wear everything only once then throw it into one of the piles.*

While all this was going on, calls were being made. Close to the entire department was being called out.

An ambulance arrived, and the husband/shooter was whisked away. No one was assigned to go with him. He wasn't about to escape, not with his hand the way it was. A statement would have been appropriate. With the taped call to the dispatcher and the statements outside when they arrived, not to mention the rest of the evidence at the scene, it wouldn't be necessary. Plus, once he hit the ER he would be so doped up with pain killers and prepped for surgery, then a statement wouldn't have been possible. Still someone should have gone to the hospital, just in case. Who knows what he might've said in the ambulance. No one had to interrogate him, just listen and make notes. He had said plenty in the driveway, so he just might have kept talking, that didn't happen.

Orders came quickly. The first officer was to secure the front door and begin an access log. Notes were to be made as to who went into the house. A second officer was posted to the rear of the house to block entry. A third was sent to the end of the driveway to control access to the property. Reporters and curious onlookers would be arriving soon. The scene needed to be sealed. News crews that had come out for the fatal accident were now shifting to the murder scene. Danny was given the unenviable task of staying with the victim.

Chapter 22

Detective Lieutenant Snyder was on his way to the scene with two detectives. A third detective was going to the hospital. At that hour of the night, it would take them a half hour to an hour to get dressed and out the door. They would be making the necessary phone calls then driving to the scene. For Danny it was going to be a long hour standing around in a room of death. The lights in the master bedroom gave a stark glow that only made the scene more macabre. Nothing looked real. Everything looked as though it came from a low budget film where they didn't have enough money for good props and lighting.

With nothing to do but wait, Danny started making notes for his report. The house lacked any kind of decorating. There were lights; some didn't have the shades in place. There were beautiful hardwood floors with no rugs. The drapes lacked color. There just wasn't anything that gave the impression that this was a real home. Danny had seen cheap motels that were more skillfully decorated. Everything looked sterile like no one cared. This house was just temporary, he observed, with no commitment. No pictures, no accent colors or any type of decorations. This was a house with no personality.

He began his notes with the first officer's arrival at the scene and Brad's statement that several officers had heard.

From there he described their entry to the home and what they saw. He drew a sketch; and as he did so, he tried to figure out how the hair got in the wall. He tried to imagine the events that took place leading up to the shooting and, of course, the final act of murder. He noticed a trail of blood across the floor and out the bedroom door. *That must have been from Brad, how the hell did he hurt his hand that way? Did he try and commit suicide? Did Penny attack him with a knife?* As he made notes, he came up with more questions and few answers. He kept writing.

Danny was still making notes when Detective LT Snyder arrived. Snyder had already been briefed by the first officer on the scene who was now guarding the front door. When the Lieutenant got to the bedroom, his first question was,

"Have you touched anything?"

The answer was "No."

"Did you take any pictures?"

Again, the answer was "No."

"Do you have a cell phone with a camera?" The question was more like a demand.

"Yes, I do, I didn't use it," said Danny.

The Lieutenant held out his hand.

"Open it up, I have to check. I don't want any of this out on the internet."

Being a rookie and a former Marine, Danny quickly and unquestioningly complied. Danny opened the photo album app on his cell phone. The Lieutenant scanned through his pictures. Danny was glad that he was never into taking selfies or trophy shots of young ladies. Most of the photos were of Bear and water scenes. As the search of his cell phone continued, it dawned on Danny that the Lieutenant didn't trust him. The Lieutenant was going through all of his photos, not just the most recent ones. Still Danny respected the rank and position and stood by patiently waiting to get his cell phone back. He figured that once the photos were checked, he'd be out of there and would never have to look at Penny again. The plus side was the scene still was not registering as real. He knew it was Penny. Somewhere in the back of his mind, he had changed this to a training exercise. The body wasn't real. It didn't look real, so it wasn't real. Penny Worthington was real, and she was dead.

The Lieutenant handed the phone back with a grunt.

Danny took the phone and put it back in the case. He turned to leave and was stopped dead in his tracks when the Lieutenant demanded,

"Where do you think you are going?"

Danny had never been at a major crime scene before. Of course, he had never been to a murder, so he assumed that his skills and ability would not be needed. Unfortunately for Danny they did need him. Someone had to do the dirty work. None of the detectives wanted to get their hands bloody. The detectives made a sketch of the scene. They then placed photo identifying numbers next to pieces of evidence. This was followed by taking photos of the items in place. Long distance shots of the room were done showing the layout of the room. Then close ups of every item to be taken as evidence. Danny then had the unenviable task of collecting the piece of evidence, making sure it was properly tagged and placed in an evidence bag for later processing.

For the next several hours Danny waited with the evidence bags until he was told which item needed to be picked up. More than 100 items were seized. There were what appeared to be slug fragments that were scattered on the floor and in the wall. There were the individual pieces of skull and hair that needed to be picked up. There were the blood splatters that needed to be swabbed for testing. The work was slow and steady. Danny tried to concentrate on the job at hand. Working so close to someone he knew who was now dead made it that much more difficult.

A Medical Examiner had been called and was allowed in to check the body. Prior to his arrival, Lieutenant Snyder directed that the body to be moved. The sheet and blanket were removed so that the Medical Examiner could inspect the entire body for the cause of death. He needed to check for any other injuries. Slowly Danny and one of the detectives removed the twisted sheet and blanket as a second detective took photographs. As Danny suspected, she was naked underneath the sheet. Her body was still warm. You could not miss the massive wound to the left rear of her head. From the right side she looked perfectly normal. Danny felt guilty staring at this naked girl who was going to wake up any second and slap him for being a pervert staring at her naked body. Of course, there was no way she was going to wake up. That didn't stop Danny from feeling guilty.

Finally, the Medical Examiner arrived. After a brief check of the body he decided that he had seen enough. More pictures had been taken. The Medical Examiner departed. Penny was gently laid in a body bag and transported to the State Medical Examiners Officer for autopsy.

Danny was glad that Penny was now out of the room. There was still work to be done. There wasn't much in the way of conversation, just directions and instructions as everyone moved about the room performing their tasks. At some point Danny realized that the Detective Lieutenant wasn't in the room.

"Where's the Lieutenant?" Danny asked.

"He had to make some phone calls," was the reply from one of the detectives.

111

"Oh," said Danny and thought nothing more of it.

They had processed everything in the room except for the wall. There was the large blast hole about five feet off the floor. The long brown hair was hanging out the opening. A red halo of blood surrounded the massive hole. There was Penny's outline in blood. It was a portrait of a young woman in death. Photos were taken of the wall from several angles. They were about to cut the sheet rock when Danny said,

"Hey, don't you think we should take a look at where the slug went? It had to come out somewhere."

The two detectives and Danny moved up to the wall, careful not to stand in the blood or brains. They looked at the black hole in the wall past the hair. A flashlight was directed into the hole.

Danny examined the hole with his flashlight rotating it around and finally centering it in the hole.

"I'm not sure; I think it goes all the way through. The insulation is all torn up, so it isn't really clear."

"Shine your light in the hole" said the detective with the camera as he stepped to the window. "Now move it around some."

Sure enough, there was the flicker of the flashlight from time to time out in the woods as Danny moved the flashlight.

"We are going to have to get a lazar in here and track the slug," said the Detective. "It has to be out there somewhere in the trees."

The Detective snapped a few photos. As this was going on, Lieutenant Snyder reappeared.

"What are you doing?" he asked.

Without thinking or hesitating, Danny stated, "Checking the slug path. It appears that the slug entered the sheet rock and went through the insulation, the plywood and blasted out through the siding into the woods." Danny gestured to the marks on the white painted dry wall that was splattered with blood and brains.

"Oh, so now you're a big-time Detective," the Lieutenant pronounced. "You're done here, sign out."

Danny took one last look at the bed, the floor, the walls and the place where he had found Penny's lifeless form. It still wasn't real. He walked out of the room for the last time.

Danny got into his cruiser and realized just how tired he was. Drained was more like it. There had been days like this in the Marines where you felt like you didn't have one ounce of energy left. The very sad and tragic thought was that he knew almost everyone directly or indirectly that he had dealt with tonight. There was no logical reason for any of it. *What could Penny have done to rate a slug in the head? What if those kids hadn't been rat-racing? Or the group crossing the street had been a little sooner in crossing or ten seconds later? Then three people would still be alive.* Danny kept trying to get an understanding out of all the nonsense. Life is a puzzle, the pieces are supposed to fit. There should have been some logic to it all. Danny couldn't help but think of all the randomness.

This was a big piece to a puzzle that Danny didn't know was coming together, or that he was going to be the center of it. As far as Danny knew, he had played only very small parts in all events of the last several hours. He wasn't the lead investigator on any of this, just part of the response. He was one of the arresting officers in the fatal. The people who would be doing the testifying would be the Reconstructionist Team, not him. The Detectives and the Lieutenant would be the ones, to make the case in Penny's death. He would have his part, filling in the details. He was just not the center of the case. One never knows the direction life will take. It seems planned and organized right up until things fall apart. People think they know what's going to happen. Danny was no exception.

Chapter 23

Danny drove to the station. He made his way inside contemplating several hours of report writing ahead of him. While he was not the lead investigator for the triple fatal, he still had to document his part. Then there were the arrests for the three breaking into the cars. Of course, there was Penny. While the three mutts breaking into the cars was not a major case, chances were good that they would not make bond, even a low one. The court would need reports for their arraignment Monday morning. This was going to be a long two days. He was trying to put his thoughts together. He was staring at the computer screen when Lieutenant Lincoln Cornell interrupted him and demanded, "What the hell were you thinking?"

Danny heard the words, they didn't register. Yes, he was tired. His head was spinning from everything that had happened. For the life of him, he could not figure out what he had done to hear a challenge like that. In the few brief seconds he was given to respond, Danny thought it might be transporting the young lady with her leg up over her shoulder. He had made the recommendation. The call was the paramedics decision not his, they had the final say. The interrogation without Miranda had already been addressed. It had to be the murder scene with Penny, but what? Then he found out.

"You moron," came the statement from LT Cornell. "You handcuffed three juveniles. Then while still cuffed, you pushed them into a cell and locked the door."

The statement hit Danny like a slap.

"Those three assholes were juveniles? They had a car, beer, drugs and a few thousand dollars' worth of stuff they had stolen. Once we got them inside the station, we got the call for the shooting. We all headed out. It never occurred to me they were juveniles. They didn't look or act that young. They never mentioned their ages."

"Well, it was your job to ask and find out. The department stands a good chance of getting sued, and so do you. A recommendation is going to court that they cut a deal with the three to not bring a lawsuit and the charges will be dropped."

Danny could not believe his ears. It had been an honest mistake. It was not an intentional act. No one planned to violate these three mutts' civil rights. Now LT Cornell was going to kick them loose and have the charges dropped. "Where are the three now?" Danny asked.

"They were released to one of the parents."

"One parent; why not to each of their parents?"

"We could only locate one mother to come in."

Danny shook his head, they had three little hoodlums breaking into cars, stealing whatever they could find, drinking beer, smoking dope and who knows what else—and they were going to get a pass. All because he and everyone else didn't have the time to ask how old they were. Three young people are dead. A young lady with a shotgun slug to her head, and three assholes get to skate. Now this lazy ass Lieutenant that never leaves the building has the balls to question their actions, Danny's actions. This sucked, and Danny was ready to let go with all barrels. He was dead tired and had seen way too much in the past few hours to let it pass. Here is this guy in a nice clean uniform with shined shoes and hair just so passing judgement. Danny was a mess inside and out. His uniform had blood from five different people staining it. The sweat stains turned his shirt a two-tone color. The mud and grass stains covered his knees from working on the young lady who was nearly cut in half, and still managed to stay alive. Danny was trying to figure out where to start and how to put this, goody-two-shoes in his place. That would be his only saving grace. He couldn't find the strength, energy, or words to respond. The anger was there. The frustration was there. The explosion was just under the surface waiting to blow any second. The bulldozer of events had just been too much on him. He could not figure out where to start or how to respond. As he collected his thoughts and formed the words he was going to say, the Lieutenant spun on his heel. With a final comment about rookies, he retreated back to his office and his cup of coffee that was getting cold.

Danny walked into the roll call room thinking of all the things he could have said, should have said. He had too much to do and wanted to get the details down before his foggy brain gave out from fatigue.

He grabbed some water and sat down at the docking stations and set up the computer so that he could dictate his report. The dictation software was much better than his typing. Still he had to think of a sentence before he dictated it to make sure it came out right. Using the keyboard, Danny entered all the heading information as to date, time, location and the officers he knew that were involved. Then he entered the suspect and the victims' names. With disbelief he wondered what the hell had gone this wrong. He then started with the narrative of the report. It had taken him over an hour

117

to get to this point since he had arrived at the station. As he began to dictate, Detective Lieutenant Snyder walked by and heard him talking into the computer. The Lieutenant halted behind Danny and listened for a minute.

Danny was concentrating on the details when he was interrupted by Detective Lieutenant Snyder.

"What the hell are you doing?" he demanded.

Danny, not knowing anyone was there, snapped around. Seeing it was Lieutenant Snyder, he flatly stated,

"Dictating my report, Sir."

"Leave out the details about the scene. The Bureau will take care of that. I just want you to put down your arrival, securing the scene, and then when you departed. We will take care of the details."

"What about what I did? Doesn't that need to be documented?"

"We will do the details," was the terse reply. "I don't want conflicting information in the facts. This is the Bureau's investigation, not Patrols. We have it, and it will be done my way."

Danny was conflicted. He wanted to get it all down on paper. Now being told he didn't have to spend the next couple of hours talking to the computer sounded too good to be true. The dirty look the Detective Lieutenant was giving him stopped the protest he was about to make. He had already pissed off one Lieutenant—why make it a twofer. Why not call it a day? Go home, take a long hot shower, and try and forget just how screwed up life can get.

"Yes Sir," Danny said, as the Detective Lieutenant disappeared down the hall.

Danny wrapped things up and headed for the door. *I still have several pages of notes and the sketch of the crime scene just in case someone asks me a question six months from now.* He was deep in thought as he headed for the Jeep and a long shower. Pictures would have helped. He didn't have to worry about having his own pictures. The detectives had taken hundreds of pictures and had 20 or more minutes of video. The nice thing about digital was that after taking the picture you could look to see what the camera had actually captured. That way there was no question whether you got the shot you wanted. Without a picture to remind him, the image of Penny staring up from the floor naked wasn't going to be erased any time soon if ever.

As the days came and went, the detectives continued their investigation. Most of it was personally handled by Detective Lieutenant Snyder. No one in the department knew what they were finding out as everyone from the Bureau wasn't permitted to say anything. There were almost no leaks. All that was coming out was that people in town heard about the rumors of the two being swingers. The leaks were not really leaks as the information was coming from the citizens. People had heard that the police had interviewed so and so and what they suspected. Officers had asked the detectives about it, and they were tight lipped. They gave very little away. When they were asked about the swinging, the detectives wanted to know where they had gotten that information. They seemed concerned that there might be a leak. No one asked the Detective Lieutenant anything, everyone knew better. Things were starting to come out in a roundabout way. People were being interviewed, and sometimes they talked. Other times the detectives would appear for an interview, and they would be seen by the civilians. People would put two and two together. They didn't always get it right. Their two cents would come up in a conversation. The speculation would grow. People were starting to have to explain why they were interviewed by the police to their friends. While the Detective Lieutenant could keep a pretty tight lid on his own people, what the public had to say and speculate on was out of his hands.

Chapter 24

Brad's hand was a mess. The medical records indicated that he had severe damage to his hand and wrist. He had shattered the bones and had torn a large jagged hole next to his thumb. The injury required several surgeries to repair what had been done. In that time, a warrant for his arrest had been issued. Detective Lieutenant Snyder served the warrant personally to Brad while he was still in the hospital. Everyone in the department and the town waited for his release from the hospital. Then the department would take custody of the suspect. He would be photographed, fingerprinted, and processed. Then there would be a bail hearing. The reporters both local and regional called almost every day waiting for the announcement that Brad was being processed and when the standard "Perp Walk" would take place. That never happened.

What did happen was that several weeks after the murder Danny spotted a one-page press release in the Dispatch Center. It was one of the shortest press releases he had ever seen. For a brutal murder of young lady, it was less than most disorderly conduct arrests.

Bradford Worthington, age 27, has been arrested in connection with the death of his wife, Penelope Worthington, age 27. Bail was posted, and the suspect has been released pending his next court appearance in Berkshire Superior Court.

Danny read it and re-read it and came up with a dozen questions. He turned to the Dispatcher for answers.

"When did this come out?"

"No idea, it was here when I came on duty."

"When was he processed?"

"No one knows."

"What was his bond?"

"No clue."

"What the hell?"

"No shit."

The Bradford Worthington family had been in town for a very long time, maybe even four generations. They were not the New York/New Jersey weekenders or the recently rich, *I have to get a country place in the Berkshires* type. This was an old trucking family that had vehicles on Interstate 90 or 91 passing by constantly. There was money in the family; more important, there were connections going back a long way.

"This stinks," said Danny to no one in particular, "this really sucks. Well, his day in court is coming, and I don't think the connections go all the way to Superior Court. There will be the news crews and real interviews."

It seemed like Penny was no longer important and just a thing from the past that people had to get beyond. Her brutal murder for still some unknown reason was taking a back seat to protecting one of the town's sons.

Weeks passed, and there was very little going on with the case on the surface. Court dates had come and gone with each appearance being continued. Several of the continuances were granted because the suspect was still undergoing medical treatment. He could not assist in his own defense because of the pain medication he was taking and the treatments he was going through. So far Brad Worthington had never set foot in the court room. No one was sure if he was ever in the police station.

When Danny was off duty and the court date was scheduled, he would make his way up to Pittsfield to be present and hear what was going on. This was on his own time as the department was not about to pay him unless he was under subpoena. What surprised Danny was that he didn't hear anything about the case. He would sit there sometimes for hours only to hear the case called and then the request for a two-week continuance. "We have a doctor's letter," the attorney would announce, and then it was over for the day.

Danny would stand outside the old court house on East Street in Pittsfield and admired the pristine landscaping and the shade trees. The court house itself was an imposing granite structure keeping in the old New England tradition of creating a stately and rock-solid impression. As he gazed at the building, he wondered if Brad would ever see the inside of this court house. Looking back, it seemed a like slam dunk that Brad would be in this court house, found guilty, and receive some serious time for killing Penny. Danny couldn't imagine what Penny had done that was so egregious to justify a shotgun slug to the head. What transgression could she have committed to warrant a death sentence? What threat did a naked female in bed pose to that nut case? When was justice going to be served? When?

Chapter 25

He could not believe it, Maidstone was getting to him. Everyone was asking him questions, and he couldn't answer. For one thing, he was sworn to secrecy, also he had no idea what was going on. Even if he could, he wasn't going to talk about finding Penny in the bedroom and what had happened in there. It was none of their business. If it came out in court, well, that was for the court to decide, not him.

Danny decided to get away for a few days and made a phone call to a State Trooper he knew and asked if she wanted to go backpacking around Stowe, Vermont. Both had middle of the week days off. With a vacation day or two thrown in, they could enjoy the mountains without the Saturday/Sunday crowd of college kids and weekend warriors. It was nice to have a companion besides Bear to go along. It was even better that she was cute and female. On the plus side she didn't have a problem carrying her own pack. They had been out on a few dates which were more like outings than what people would call a date. They would hike the trails in the Berkshires and go for runs. Danny could run circles around her, though it was much better to run behind her and let her set the pace. The view was better, and he enjoyed watching her blonde ponytail going up and down and side to side keeping pace with her stride. Yes, the view was much better from behind.

It hadn't been a love-at-first-sight type thing. Looking back, getting a date with her almost ended on the very first try. Danny had been on a day off and was about to head out of the barn when he got a text message to respond with his gear to Route 9 south of town for a suspect in the woods. He jumped in the Jeep and headed south and found a bunch of cruisers from town and from Great Barrington.

"What have we got?" asked Danny.

Lieutenant Cornell told him that there had been a stolen car chase and a possible armed robbery down in Connecticut with shots fired. The suspects had bailed out and ran into the wooded swampy area just east of Route 9. Two of the suspects had run head long into the swamp only to find a pool five or six feet deep. They went under and came up spitting water and cursing. With all their clothes on soaking up then water, they nearly drowned. One officer was right there and took the two into custody. They thought there was still a third suspect out there. Other units were positioned on the far side in a blocking position. The first units on the scene had called the State Police for a tracking dog. They had been told that it was in route.

"Danny," Lieutenant Cornell stated, "I want you to go with the State Police K-9 unit on the track when they arrive and it should be here shortly. You have the most experience hunting down people, and this is right up your alley."

As the Lieutenant was saying this, units were leaving the area and heading into other blocking positions on the surrounding roads. Some were taking up posts over a mile away to cut off any possible avenue of escape. Danny wasn't too keen on being considered a man hunter. He did have more experience in this line of work. He was also amazed that Lieutenant Cornell was actually out of the office. His presence at the scene terminated as soon as he relayed his instructions to Danny. He was out of there and headed back to the station.

"Will do," said Danny as the LT disappeared and he waited for the State Police to arrive. It was a somewhat cold night for the Berkshires and Danny moved around in part to keep warm and partly out of nervousness. The longer they waited, the more time the suspect had to find a way through the perimeter or to set up an ambush for anyone following him. Danny didn't have too much time to wait as a State Police cruiser pulled in. Danny walked over to the cruiser, no one got out. He looked in the back window and didn't see a tracking dog. He opened the passenger's side door and asked to get in. A female voice said *"sure,"* and this is how Danny met Trooper Geraldine Anyzeski. Danny made some small talk and took a second glance into the back seat just to confirm that there wasn't a dog there. Maybe the dog was on the floor, and he couldn't see it from the outside. Still, there was no dog. Impatient to get going and wondering where the dog was he asked, "So where's your dog?"

The testy reply was, "I don't need a dog."

Now Danny was at a total loss. He had been told that the State Police were sending a tracking dog and that he should go with them. He was trying to figure out what to do or what to ask next. His last question was not received all that well. While she looked kinda cute, she also had an attitude. Danny ran things through his mind. *We asked for a dog, they sent her. Well, okay,* Danny thought, *what kind of a nose does she have and when is she going to get out of the car?* Fortunately, before Danny could make matters worse, a State Police SUV pulled up. A Trooper got out followed by a big old slobbering bloodhound. Danny came to the quick conclusion that this was the tracking team and not the female State Trooper with an attitude. He excused himself and exited the cruiser. Not being the shy type, he couldn't help but ask, "Would you like to go out sometime?"

Without missing a beat or even a moment's thought an immediate reply was, "No."

Danny headed over to introduce himself to the Trooper with the bloodhound. Being a trained observer, he did get a quick look at her name tag. Now all he had to do was try and remember it. Of course, it couldn't have been Smith or Brown, no it had to be Anyzeski. All he had to do now was try to and remember the correct spelling.

"Hi, Danny Gilcrest; I'll be going on the track with you." All he got was a grunt from the dog handler. He had a clear look at the handler and then kept looking back and forth at the bloodhound and the handler. They looked like brothers—sad, droopy eyes, a long-wrinkled face, big ears, a little slobber in the corner of the mouth, and they both smelled. *This is going to be a fun night. First, a female Trooper with an attitude and now two bloodhounds to go for a walk with— one with four legs and one with two legs, neither one seemed to speak English.*

"All right," the dog handler began with what sounded like a slow southern drawl. "I ain't gunna be able to have my gun out as I have to be usin both my hands to hold the dog back. We're gunna be on a 15-foot leash; and if she's tracking, then she's gunna be pullin. So, I gotta hang on tight. I want you off to my right with the shotgun to cover me. Whatever you do, don't get in front of the dog."

Danny nodded his understanding, checked the shotgun, and was ready to move out. The female Trooper never got out of her cruiser. *Oh well, next time,* he thought.

The dog was given time to check out the scents in the stolen vehicle. Then it was off to the races in slow motion. Into the woods and swamp, they went with the dog pulling the handler through all kinds of brush. They could see where the first two suspects had gone, and the dog was right on their scent. The area was recently flooded, probably from some beaver activity. The woods were a mess of downed trees, green briers and fallen branches. It was also dark. They passed the place where the two suspects had tried to drown themselves in their well-planned escape and they continued on deeper into the woods. The handler told Danny that the way the dog was pulling meant they were on to something. Danny, already wired, became even more vigilant if that were possible. Several times the dog would suddenly stop pulling. Danny would bring the shotgun up level and scan the area wondering what had caused the dog to stop. Just as fast, the dog would start pulling again. They would be at a slow trot once more. Then the dog froze in place. Danny sensed that danger was near. He moved forward with the shotgun at the ready looking for movement to the front. The front turned out to be the least of Danny's worries. Like lightning, the lack-luster bloodhound struck like a rattlesnake. Danny, concentrating on what was in front, never saw it coming. In the blink of an eye, the bloodhound had the fly of Danny's trousers in his mouth. There was no bark, no growl, just a flash of a move. Danny gasped, wondering if there was anything left. Fortunately, he felt no pain, only the hard tug on the cotton material. As fast as it happened, the bloodhound let go and went back to being a slobbering bum. Danny was breathing hard; still not sure of what had happened. He was hoping that his future love life might still have a chance. He looked down. Other than a few teeth marks on his trousers, everything seemed to be intact. Danny looked at the dog and then at his twin, the handler, he couldn't think of anything to say. The dog handler looked back at him in disgust. He shook his head and mumbled, "I told ya not to get in front of the dog."

Danny looked at the slobbering handler, the equally slobbering bloodhound, and his slightly damaged trousers. He nodded his head and said "Yes." *He would definitely remember the warning from now on.*

They kept up their search for close to an hour covering all kinds of nasty ground looking for the third suspect. There was thought to be a third guy in part because no one saw how many suspects there were running from the vehicle, and the fact was that these guys had always in the past operated as a team of three. So there had to be a third suspect.... that is, until they found out that the Three Amigos were down to the Two Amigos. The Third was in Whalley Ave Jail in New Haven, Connecticut, for assault.

Danny and the two bloodhounds, human and K-9, exited the woods. By this time Danny looked like the other two including the smell. He would never be considered a neat freak, but now he was trying to figure out how to get into his Jeep without turning it into a mobile swamp complete with water, mud, and vegetation.

Danny got an evidence bag and took off as many cloths and footwear as possible still remaining legally clothed in the eyes of the law and the citizens of the beautiful and tranquil Berkshires. Half-naked, he drove home freezing off what the bloodhound had almost removed. As he entered the barn, he took off the few remaining articles of clothing at the door. He threw them on the lawn and made a dash for the shower. Bear gave him a curious look. The smell got to Bear, and Danny nearly had company in the shower. He scrubbed for what seemed like forever. Then he exited the shower, wrapped a towel around himself, and headed for the refrigerator. He grabbed a Sam Adams and went to the easy-chair and collapsed. Bear was still curious, and now he was checking to see what had happened to that smell. After a full search of Danny's body, he gave up and with a humph, dropped down at Danny's feet and went to sleep. The TV was on tuned to the Antiques Road Show. He got about two sips of beer and saw one painting being appraised. The next thing he knew it was six hours later. The beer was still in his hand, and Bear was nudging him awake for breakfast. Bear could tolerate a lot of things, missing a meal was not one of them.

Danny actually felt good despite being physically drained. Of course, they didn't make a good grab; still he loved the intensity of the evening. He was also thankful that he came home with everything he left with. He looked at Bear and thought thank God I can walk in front of you without worrying about the consequences. Bear smiled and nudged him one more time to remind him that breakfast was already late.

Slowly Danny began to move, got Bear's breakfast and made some coffee.

What was that female Trooper's name, he asked himself? *I may be looking for trouble; hopefully there was something there besides the serious attitude.*

Chapter 26

Meeting Geri again in Ski Patrol class helped to ease things. Danny persisted, and finally got to go out with her, sort of. He had the first aid skills down pat and could do the rope work needed to get skiers off a stalled chairlift in his sleep. He was also fairly large in size so that handling a toboggan by himself wasn't a problem. Now skiing was another thing. Danny was a good average skier. Geri could ski circles around him and just about anyone else, any time she liked. When winter came, Danny would do the dirty work and the heavy lifting and let Geri show the tourists what great skiers the ski patrol were. For now, Danny would have to settle for runs, hikes sometimes, a beer and a sandwich after. Most people would not call what they were doing a date. He found out that she didn't have an attitude most of the time and that she could be quite pleasant when she wanted. Bear was probably Danny's biggest asset. If he kept his mouth shut and let Bear do the schmoozing, the encounters were always positive. Eventually, Bear would have to let him take his chances and succeed or fail on his own. So long as Bear was in the picture, Danny was golden or at least not like some other asshole he had heard about that Geri had dated.

The drive up was easy, taking Route 100 most of the way to Stowe. On the way, they stopped off for an early dinner at the Long Trail Inn, a very classy place that lost some of its old stately charm when they remodeled the inside. The outside still looked much the same though cleaned up to exacting Vermont standards. The inside had a new, modern Yuppie look and feel. There was still some nice old wood paneling, but it had lost that old worn New England charm.

They ate dinner and then moved up the road to Smugglers' Notch State Park where they set up a base camp. There were roomy tent sites, and the bathrooms were new and very clean. For a couple of quarters, you could get a hot shower and wash all the sweat from a day's hiking off and feel like a new man or, in Geri's case, woman. This time of the year and midweek the park was almost empty. There was plenty of space between the few people who were there. On the plus side was the fact that there wasn't anyone there for a camping/beer party. The idea of getting away was just that, to get away from the drunks, the job, and the noise. This was Danny's idea of getting away, not some booze/eating contest on a cruise to the Bahamas. Fortunately for Danny, Geri thought this was a good idea too.

Geri had been with the State Police for a few years, and their paths had crossed several times. Some of those meetings were by accident and some completely intentional on Danny's part. At first, she wasn't at all sure about going camping with a police officer and a former Marine. She pictured sleeping under a poncho eating spam out of a can and getting up at 5 AM. Then there would be an 18 mile hike up hill all the way. Danny assured her that it would be nothing like that. Yes, he had been a Marine and had roughed it many times, too many times. Now he didn't have to rough it so why beat yourself up when this can be an enjoyable experience. When Geri heard that Bear was coming along, she knew that it would be less of a death march that she feared. Danny would never do anything that would harm Bear. He took better care of Bear than he did himself. If this trip was good enough for Bear, then it was good enough for her. She loved Bear; Danny was still a work in progress. Time would tell.

They both slept in the dome tent, and Bear was the unofficial chaperone. The yellow lab took his third out of the middle getting part of his body on Danny's sleeping pad and the rest on Geri's. There he settled in tucked securely between the two. Danny put his down jacket over him to keep him warm.

As Danny dozed off, all he could think about was, here he is in northern Vermont with a lovely young lady who he had just had dinner with. They were now tucked into a tiny tent, and his Labrador was snuggling closer to her than he was. *Life is so unfair.* Then again, there is tomorrow.

Tomorrow, while without prior satisfaction, was still shaping up to be a good day. Danny made some fresh brewed coffee. They had whole wheat bagels with peanut butter and some fruit for breakfast. They headed out and made their way to Taft Lodge on the northeast side of Mount Mansfield.

Chapter 27

Geri took one look at Taft Lodge and remarked, "This isn't a hut; this is a cabin. There's a porch and windows, and it's totally enclosed." It was a few miles from the road tucked into the side of the mountain and close to absolutely nothing.

Danny, a little taken aback asked, "You want this to be more rustic? This isn't roughing it enough for you?"

"No, not at all, this is fine. I just didn't know that any of the huts were this nice. I was thinking of the three-side shelters, this is a full-size cabin."

"Well, there's no running water except for the brook over there. If you have to do Number 1 or Number 2, you still have to go outside."

Geri marveled at the place. It had been re-done in 1998 and was a far cry from the real old barn of a place that it had once been. The Long Trail Club had re-built this place right. It was solid and beautiful. It wasn't a resort. It was a safe, dry location with water nearby and with a drop dead gorgeous view when there wasn't any fog. Today was one of those 100-mile vistas. The fall colors of the trees just lit up the valley. The yellows from the birch trees and the reds from the maples mixed in with the greens of the pines painted a beautiful scene. In the distance, you could see the white church steeple in the center of the town poking above the trees.

"We will be bunking here tonight," Danny announced, "so we can dump the big packs in the lodge. I have a small day pack for what we will need for the rest of today."

Geri had been thinking on the way up about hauling all their gear to the top. That would be several miles more. Now, after a short hike in, they were dropping most of the weight. *Was this guy really a Marine?*

"Sort through what you want to take to the top, and I will put it in the day pack. Make sure you have a warm layer and a windbreaker for up there, it gets pretty windy on most days." As she sorted through her stuff, Danny headed out the door. She didn't see the zip lock bag in his hand concealed behind his leg.

"Where are you going?"

"I want to check the stream and make sure we have a good flow of water. Whatever you do, don't drink from the streams around here; there is always a chance of getting giardia and that can be real nasty." He was only gone for a few minutes and quickly re-appeared having accomplished his task. Geri handed him her windbreaker and tied a polar fleece around her waist. She then handed Danny a Clinique bag with some items in it.

"Don't drop that," she cautioned.

As soon as Danny touched the bag he knew why. Among several items in the bag, he felt the distinct outline of a snub-nosed revolver.

"Really, a revolver as an off-duty piece, I thought you would have a small automatic?"

"That was my father's off-duty weapon, and I still carry it. That was the first handgun I ever fired, and I like it. At close range I don't miss."

"I will keep that in mind," as he loaded the items into the pack. They headed out and up for an even more spectacular view.

Even without heavy packs, it was a good climb up. The hike was worth it. They found a sheltered spot, and Danny dug out lunch which consisted of nuts, some cheese, French bread, and some summer sausage. Bear got most of the sausage. They washed it down with a small bottle of gator aid. They explored the top of Mount Mansfield and took dozens of pictures. Then as the sun was starting to dip, they made their way back down to Taft Lodge.

On the trail, they crossed a small, well flowing stream. The water cascading down had worn the rocks smooth and had carved out several bathtub-like pools in the granite.

Geri looked at one of the larger pools that were about the size of a six-person hot tub.

"You know I feel kinda sticky and sweaty from the climb up. Do you mind if we stop and go skinny dipping to get cleaned up?"

Danny wasn't sure he had actually heard what she had said. Was she really asking him permission to get naked and go for a dip? Was he invited? Was he supposed to move down the trail and wait for her? While all these thoughts were going through his head, Geri started taking off her clothes. *Well, I guess that answers that.*

Danny would never be considered a prude, but this quick decision to get naked and go for dip was happening faster than he could adjust. *Maybe she was into doing the wild thing in a wild environment. Who knows? If she asks you to get naked, why fight it.* Danny began to strip.

Geri slipped into the pool first and Danny had all kinds of expectations about what was going to happen in the pool. Geri wasn't a big buxom girl, more of an athletic type body — someone who hit the gym everyday which wasn't a bad thing. This was going to be interesting, Danny thought right up until he slipped into the water. Any chances of romance went out the window as the freezing cold water sent everything below the waist line looking for a place to hide. The sudden rush was a shock taking his breath away. He wondered if he would ever see his family jewels again. After a few seconds, he was able to breathe normally, though nothing else was reappearing. Still, he was in a mountain stream with a lovely young lady naked as can be. This was a plus though he wasn't sure where to go from here.

"I just love skinny dipping," said Geri, "and I hate being dirty. I just can't resist sliding in and cooling off."

Well, thought Danny, *I wish I had known that before. I would have found some water that wasn't close to freezing and taken*

138

her there. If I had just known that she could not resist water and had to get naked.

As they sat there freezing in the splashing water, Bear was watching them and edging to get in.

"No Bear—get. The last thing we need is a wet dog to snuggle with tonight."

Then they noticed that Bear was no longer trying to get in or even looking at them. Bear was facing them, looking over their shoulders past them staring back up the trail. Slowly they both turned and looked over their shoulders to see a half dozen Boy Scouts up on the trail staring at the naked people in the pool. The Scouts couldn't see anything, that didn't make the situation any less awkward. They slipped a little lower into the cold water. They were just about to get out when they were discovered by the Scouts. The cold water, after feeling somewhat refreshing, was now just too damn cold. They couldn't get out without a full flash for the Boy Scouts. After what seemed like a cold, torturous lifetime, one of the Scout leaders made his way up to the group of astonished Scouts and figured out what the holdup was. He began shooing the boys up the trail, but not before he took a good look himself. As the cold water began to turn their lips blue, all Danny could think about was the headline in the morning paper: *State Trooper and local officer expose themselves to a Boy Scout Troop on the Long Trail. Disciplinary action and possible termination hearings are pending.*

As the Boy Scouts disappeared up the trail, the two shivering, embarrassed police officers scrambled out of the pool, pulled their cloths on, and beat feet down the trail.

Chapter 28

They relaxed a bit at the lodge, broke out the sleeping bags and mats, and retrieved the backpacker headlights before it got too dark to find them. As the sun began to fade behind the mountain, Danny began to prepare dinner. He retrieved the zip lock bag from the stream. Fortunately, no critters had gotten into it or they might not have a dinner to look forward to.

"Well, Jarhead, what's for dinner, MREs?"

"Linguini with white clam sauce," was the quick response.

She assumed he was joking until Danny pulled two small cans of clams out of his pack and began to open them.

"Really; Linguini with white clam sauce; no appetizer?" she kidded.

"Oh shit, I forgot."

Danny reached into the zip lock bag and pulled out two nippers of scotch. He then handed her a small stainless-steel cup that had been chilled sitting in the stream water.

"Here is your before-dinner cocktail. It is chilled, sorry, no ice." He turned over the nipper and went back into the bag a came out with two small jars of the pre-made shrimp cocktails with sauce included also chilled from the stream.

Geri was surprised and at the same time thought of the ingenuity to come up with these little perks. Backpacking wasn't going to be Marine Corps style.

Danny got the single burner backpacker stove going. In a small pie-plate-like pan, he put in some butter and crushed garlic. When the butter melted, he added the clam juice and just a bit of flour to thicken the juice into a sauce, to which he added the clams. Once everything was heated up, Danny put a pot of water on the stove and put the pie plate on top to keep the clams warm. When the water boiled, in went the linguini. Danny and Geri sat on the porch sipping scotch, eating shrimp cocktail and admiring the view.

So far no one else had shown up at Taft Lodge to spend the evening. This is the most beautiful time of the year, and there was no one on the mountain. Even the Boy Scout Troop had gone someplace else. This wasn't Danny's plan, though he had to admit, it was working.

Danny had Geri check the linguini to make sure it achieved the tenderness to her liking. When she proclaimed the pasta done, Danny rinsed it off and then added the clam sauce to the mix. He then produced some oregano, parsley, and grated cheese for a topping.

There was one more surprise for Geri as Danny served the pasta dinner. He pulled out a Poland Spring water bottle. Geri was pleased that they had clean fresh water that wasn't tainted. Then Danny put two additional shiny stainless-steel cups on the bench. He poured the water, which Geri noticed that had a slight yellow tint to it.

"What's this?" she asked with suspicion in her voice.

"Sauvignon Blanc from Chile, it's a bit dry. I hope you like it because we have a very limited wine list."

Geri took a sip and thought that this was a very remarkable Jarhead. Scotch, shrimp cocktail, linguini with white clam sauce and now a dry white wine served in a chilled cup. Now this was her idea of what backpacking should be. She didn't know it could be like this until now.

They finished dinner and moved out on to the porch to watch the stars come out and the moon to come up.

After a while Danny went back in to the lodge and came out with something in his hand. In the dim light Geri couldn't make it out so she asked the obvious question, "What's that?"

"Desert." Danny broke a six-inch soft chocolate chip cookie in half and gave Geri one side. "Amaretto, Grand Marina or Baileys?" he asked.

"Baileys of course," was the questioning response.

Danny handed her a nipper of Baileys and proceed to join her on the steps watching the night take over the valley and the mountain. The long shadows began to consume the valley, and the colors of autumn began to turn purple and fade to black.

Both started to doze off on the porch, and they decided it was time to turn in. Geri readied for bed while Danny tidied things up and put the packs up where the little critters wouldn't get into the food. By this time, Geri was in her sleeping bag. Bear had claimed his spot in the middle, tucked into the side of Geri's sleeping bag. It was pitch black in the lodge with the backpacker headlights giving limited lighted areas. There was a bit of a warm glow off the wood, it did not provide detail just a general view of things. Danny climbed into his bag trying to get some of the space Bear was taking up between him and Geri. He thought of re-locating Bear, then again that would have been a bit too obvious, and things were going well. He didn't want to scare her off. With the thought that the day was over, and it was time to sleep, Geri asked him a question.

142

From out of the darkness he heard,

"Hey, Danny, can I ask you something personal? You don't have to answer if you don't want to."

This caught Danny off guard and he was now on the defensive. *What could she possibly be asking him that would be phrased that way?*

"I guess so, go ahead. Ask away."

He had said it and was still concerned as to what was coming next. Most questions could just be asked and not qualified in such a manner.

"Are you gay?"

Danny was floored and wondering what on earth had he done to raise that issue. He gave a long, emphasized drawn out,

"NOOOOO."

"Then why am I snuggling with Bear and not you?"

OH shit; here I am trying to play it cool and slow and I have to be directed to step up. Trying to find a quick and witty reply Danny said,

"I thought you liked Bear better than me."

"I do, I do, that doesn't mean WE can't snuggle a little."

Danny re-positioned an uncooperative 70-pound Bear to another location and put his parka over him. He then rolled over close to Geri. In the dark, he put his arm out to hold her close. When he did, he intended to go over the sleeping bag. Instead his hand went inside her bag, and it was then he realized she was once again naked. His hand touched warm soft flesh, and it felt so inviting. At the same time, he was about to yank his hand back as fast as he could, not wanting to get a punch in the mouth. He realized that she hadn't pulled away. In fact, she had scooted closer up to him and molded into his body.

"Rub my back please, it's a little sore."

143

Danny gently began to rub her back. As time went on he began moving his hand in larger circles going higher and lower and from side to side. His exploring brought no protests only contented sighs and soft purring like sounds. He continued to rub getting closer to danger zones, and still there was no resistance. The effects of the icy plunge that afternoon had worn off, and everyone south on the belly button was now showing a heightened interest in everything the hand was exploring. He took a chance and kissed her gently on the back of the neck which only brought more contented sounds and closer snuggling.

Chapter 29

As the sun began to peek through the windows, there was movement inside the lodge. Because of the elevation and that it faced east, the cabin caught the sun very early. That was OK because turn in time was just after sunset. The only variation was that only Bear went right to sleep. With no one to rub his back, he lost interest quickly and dozed off. Not so for Danny and Geri. It was a tangle of sleeping bags and warm bodies as he tried to make his way to a sitting position. Sometime during the night when things had finally quieted down, Bear had made his way back into the mix. Now he lay twisted up in the sleeping bags. Bear still thought it was too early to get up and remained uncooperative in being removed from the sleeping bags. He wasn't about to give up his position of warmth and comfort without a fight. Bear's 70 pounds and the fact that he had Geri and Danny pinned did not make moving easy. Danny was looking at a sleeping Geri. Her hair was a long blonde wonderful mess, and he tried to convince himself of the nights past events—or was he just very wishfully thinking. Geri saw him looking down at her, gave him a big smile followed by a long deep kiss. Then there was an unqualified demand for coffee.

Danny had also thought about coffee that is until the kiss. Then his thoughts went back south. Unfortunately, the demand, the order, the insistence on coffee did not sound in any way negotiable. He rolled to his side disengaging himself from Bear and the sleeping bag and found what clothes he could. He started the backpacker stove going to boil some water. Geri pulled the sleeping bag and Bear closer and informed him to wake her when the coffee was done.

A take-charge person, he thought, "Coffee coming up."

Danny made the coffee fresh ground with a small drip pot. There would be no instant coffee when he could make fresh brewed. The smell of the coffee filled the cold lodge with steam rising and moving through the empty structure.

The smell of the coffee brought Geri to a sitting position, and she watched as Danny poured the water over the grounds.

"For real?" she asked. "Fresh brewed coffee?"

Danny shrugged his shoulders. "Of course, it's fresh brewed. It tastes so much better, breakfast in bed for Madame?"

"And breakfast is?" she asked.

"Unfortunately, today it's going to be simple. There is apple cinnamon oatmeal, some fruit and bagels with peanut butter. I was thinking of pancakes, but figured we would eat a light breakfast and head down and get a late lunch/early dinner in Stowe."

Geri faked disappointment, truth be told that plan sounded wonderful. The hike, the dip, the dinner, the lodge, the privacy, now breakfast in bed.

"Are you sure you were in the Marines?"

"Yes," was the emphatic reply, "I have the paperwork and tee shirts to prove it."

"I heard that coffee in the morning for a Marine was ripping open one of those small instant bags of coffee and dumping it into your mouth. Then you add the packet of sugar along with the dry cream. You top it off by taking a couple of slugs of warm water and gulping it down."

"I've done that on more than one occasion. Now I don't have to.

"This is so un-Marine."

"I have had some very rough nights out. When I don't have to, there is no reason to. If I ran you up the mountain and had you carry your pack the whole time and then fed you MREs and had you sleep on the ground, would that have been better?"

"No, of course not. I just didn't expect that backpacking could be like this. Or that a Marine could come up with this take on camping. It's fine; actually, it's great. I think I might want to do it again."

"Would you be willing to do it ALL again?" Danny asked with a slight grin.

A smile came to Geri's soft sweet beautiful face.

"Maybe, it depends on the coffee."

"Well, I can't say that I thought that a Massachusetts State Trooper would be into skinny dipping or need a back rub at the end of the day."

Geri tried to make a mean Trooper face, the smile made that impossible.

"Bite me, big boy."

"Don't temp me young lady, I just might."

"Careful, I still have the snubby, and I think Bear likes me better than you."

Danny looked over, and Bear was tucked in as close to her as possible. He couldn't blame him. He wished to switch positions, but the coffee was just about done.

"Yes, ma'am, how do you take your coffee?"

147

Chapter 30

They had their coffee and bagels which they shared with Bear. Then they packed up their gear and headed down. The valley was dotted with fog that was rising from the river. It looked like someone had put big cotton balls on top of the trees, and the color between the fall foliage and the dark greens of the pines with the cotton balls mixed in made for excellent photos. They got back to the camp ground and hit the showers and changed into clean cloths. It was still shorts, tee shirts, and chamois shirts for downtown. This was Stowe, Vermont, and people in blue blazers, oxford cloth shirts, and khaki pants mixed with hikers. No one gave it a second look, it was Vermont. Their first stop was going to be the Long Trail Inn. Geri liked their signature cocktail, The Maple Tree. It was too sweet for Danny. On the plus side they had Sam Adams, and so it was all good. They parked out front in the shade with Bear left guarding the open Jeep. Before they were ten feet away, a lady asked if she could pet Bear. "Of course," said Danny, knowing what a chick magnet Bear was. If Danny had a one-year-old nephew and Bear, every female in Stowe would be at his Jeep. As it was, there was always someone—of the female persuasion anywhere between five and seventy-five years old wanting to scratch Bear's head. Bear was always completely cooperative.

As they headed up the sidewalk they saw a brand new, shiny black Cadillac Escalade with Mass plates parked in front. It looked so familiar to Danny, he just couldn't place it. *Must be some Boston type,* he thought. As they walked into the bar, Danny noticed a couple talking to the bartender. The guy had his back to Danny; the female was in profile—and what a profile it was. While Geri had the light-hard body of an athlete and the blonde hair pulled back in a casual ponytail, this young lady looked like a Playboy model with her clothes on. She had long, wavy thick dark, red hair and a fair complexion, with light green eyes. Her makeup was perfect, and her clothes made sure that every curve of her body was accentuated. Danny was more than happy to have a State Trooper with an attitude on his arm. He was not thinking that this would be trading up or that somehow the young lady at the bar was more desirable. Still he had to admit that she was hot. The bartender passed a large beer glass to the gentleman with his back to Danny and then announced, "Go easy, these Long Island Ice Teas can sneak up on you." That was when

149

Danny noticed the sling on the guy's left arm. The first though was that, *it isn't ski season yet, what happened*?

The young lady at the bar noticed Danny was looking in their direction, and the look became a pretty intense stare. The man at the bar saw his girlfriend looking behind him and following her gaze, slowly turning while holding the glass. That was when Danny and Brad Worthington locked eyes, staring deep into each other's soul. Brad began to wither under the glare; he was backed up to the bar and had no place to go. Geri and the young lady at the bar had no idea what was happening. Both knew that something had just clicked and it wasn't good. They showed faces of concern looking back and forth between themselves and the men trying to figure out who had just turned an ice-cold fire hose on the place. Even the bartender picked up on the tension. Not a word had been spoken. The look Danny was giving was brutal enough. The bartender watched the men, thinking that at any second there would be an explosion.

"Geri, we're leaving."

Geri was about to protest then saw the look, a look she had never seen before on Danny or anyone else. It spoke volumes. Geri slipped her hand into her fanny pack and fingered the snub-nose 38. She wasn't sure what was going down, the vibrations indicated that they were in danger. Something was about to happen, and it wasn't going to be good.

With eyes still locked, they made their way back to the door. The bartender was frozen in position praying that the couple would make it outside. Then this would be all over and things would go back to normal.

On the street Danny tried to shake off the tension and rage that had built up inside of him during those few seconds.

He was madder than he had ever dreamed he could get and frustrated beyond belief.

Geri kept her hand on the snubby, looking back to see that they hadn't been followed.

"What the hell was that?" she demanded.

As they walked back to the Jeep, Danny kept shaking his head trying to speak. He would begin to say something, but nothing was coming out.

Seeing Danny so agitated was unnerving to Geri. This was Mr. Calm, Cool and Collected. Now he was rendered speechless. Whatever was going on, it was serious. She kept her hand on the gun and watched the door.

"Let's go," Danny said in a very slow, subdued voice and headed to for the Jeep.

"Is that guy going to follow us?" asked a concerned Geri.

"That little maggot doesn't have the balls to follow a kindergartener."

They got in the Jeep. Danny drove a few hundred yards up the road and pulled over. He stared straight ahead for a long time not saying a word.

Geri was still trying to figure things out and thought that she should be included in what was going on. The look, the clenched jaw, the tension held her back—and then the explosion.

With an animal roar, Danny let it all out. "Son of a mother-fuckin-bitch," he yelled as his fists pounded the steering wheel. Geri was shocked, scared, and about to run. All the rage was directed at the steering wheel and some unseen person in Danny's mind. The rage passed almost as fast as it had appeared. Now Danny was slumped over exhausted. He was trying to get his breathing under control.

The past few minutes had been overload for Geri. It was sudden, intense, and totally out of character. In a soft voice somewhat frightened to know what this was all about, Geri asked once more,

"What just happened?"

Danny took several deep breaths. In a quiet, halting voice, he told her the story of Brad and Penny Worthington.

Geri listened in silence, hearing everything from the school bus rides in high school to picking up brains off the floor. Danny didn't leave out the three pedestrians and the teenager with her leg over her shoulder. He included the three juveniles breaking into cars. Danny told her everything, and it was more like he was dictating a report then talking to someone. It was detailed, complete, gruesome, and in the end devastating.

All Geri could say was, "this happened all in one night?"

"Yes."

Geri sat back in the seat and tried to comprehend everything she had just heard and what she had just witnessed. Bear knew that something was wrong and made his way forward in between the two front seats. Instinctively, they both reached down and began stroking Bear's large head and he was doing what he did best, being there and calming things down.

Like a bolt of lightning, it hit Geri.

"If he blew his wife's brains out a couple of months ago, who's the cupcake?"

Exhausted, Danny slumped further in the seat taking Bear's head in both of his hands, rubbing his ears.

"If I have my information correct that would be the psychiatrist that took care of him the night of the murder. Seems he was so traumatized by the events of the evening he needed professional help. She looks like the shrink that was described to me. I've never met her or even seen her until today."

Geri was flabbergasted.

"Is she nuts? Going with a guy that just kills his wife and you hookup in the emergency room?"

Danny looked, shrugged, and shook his head. He couldn't think of a response. He put the Jeep in gear, and they slowly headed out of town, down the road to anywhere away from the Long Trail Inn.

As they drove away, Danny was deep in thought. First thing he was going to do was report what had just happened—that a guy who was too injured to be in court could be in Stowe, Vermont, sucking down Long Island Ice Teas with a hot babe on his arm. He would like to have broken the other arm. Ratting him out was the best he could do and not get into trouble. There were too many witnesses. The second thing was that he was never going back to the Long Trail Inn.

Chapter 31

On the way back to the campground, Danny made a quick stop at a state liquor store and came out with a jug of Johnnie Walker Black and a bag of ice. Geri saw the Scotch and was about to say something, she held off making any comment. Drinking a jug of scotch, no matter how good it was, would not help anything and probably make matters worse.

When they got back to the campsite, Danny got a fire going in the small stone fireplace that each site had. They moved close to the fire, Bear included. Using the picnic table for a back rest and their sleeping pads to sit on they made themselves comfortable. Following Danny's lead, they wrapped up in the sleeping bags and watched the fire. Danny cracked open the Scotch, and asked Geri if she would like some.

A soft "no" was the only response. She was about to say something, once again she thought better of it. Danny poured a good six ounces into a cup and rested back against the picnic table. Seeing that everyone was settled in, Bear made his move selecting the one spot that appeared to be the softest and most comfortable. His decision was also based on a second important factor. He needed to be in a position where both Danny and Geri could pet him. He didn't want to play favorites and made sure that he shared himself equally. He was always very considerate that way.

They gazed at the fire stroking bear's head. Sometime later, they both drifted off to sleep. The three once more all wrapped up together.

The fire died down, and the late afternoon turned to evening. Things started to get cold causing them to stir. It was also Bear's dinner time, and he never liked missing a meal. So, Bear was checking to see who was going to get up and prepare his evening feast.

Danny rolled out of the tangle and almost knocked the cup of Scotch over. He opened the bottle. Geri was certain that he was going to pour more into the cup. To her surprise, he poured the contents of the cup back in to the bottle. He put the cap back on the bottle, setting it on the picnic table.

"Why did you do that?" a questioning Geri asked.

"I am not about to waste good scotch."

"Not that. Why did you pour the scotch in the first place?"

"Because I could."

"Why did you pour it back in and not drink it?"

"Again, because I could."

Geri hugged Bear as Danny set about getting his food ready. *This guy is just full of surprises*, thought Geri, and his dog is a love. She had been dreading what would happen after a couple of glasses of scotch. That thankfully, she never found out. She couldn't blame him if he drank the whole bottle after hearing about that night. It was a shock seeing the murderer with his new squeeze partying hearty. She hoped Danny wouldn't get hammered. It had worked itself out. Geri knew that everything was fine for right now. She also knew that type of night just doesn't evaporate and disappear in a cloud of smoke from a campfire. She just hoped that down the road it didn't drown in a bottle of Scotch.

She had to ask, "You bought the Scotch, you poured it and then you didn't drink it, why?"

"Like I said before, because I could. Before I took that first sip I really did think of tying one on. In the morning, I would feel like shit, have a serious headache, and an urge to blow lunch. That asshole would still be free, and I would be punishing myself and not him. Then while I'm contemplating making myself sick, I have a lovely young lady snuggle up to me. Then a big yellow Labrador comes over smiling, trying to find a warm place to fit in. Of course, there is the campfire warming my face. So, I am thinking, screw him, he isn't worth it. You have a problem with that?"

Geri's first reaction was one of surprise, confusion and mainly relief. "Well, if all it takes to chill you out is a little snuggling and a smiling Labrador, I think I can do my part."

"Don't forget the campfire and the sleeping bags."

"I will write that down, so I don't forget."

She came over and gave him a big hug and a huge long kiss. Danny was thinking that she might need her back rubbed again when she announced, "In case you forgot, we were supposed to have a late lunch which we passed on. Now it's getting past dinner time. How about you take me somewhere nice and feed me before I get cranky?"

Maybe a back rub later, he thought, *he hoped.*

"Not a problem, young lady. We just have to wait for Bear to finish, and we're outta here under one condition."

"Yes?"

"Keep your eyes open for a Cadillac Escalade with Massachusetts plates. If you see one that even comes close to that, we are not pulling in."

"Agreed."

As the three headed to the Jeep, Geri adjusted her fanny pack. She unconsciously moved her fingers across the bag to make sure the outline of the snubby was still there. *A murderer meets his new squeeze in the ER the night that he kills his wife. Go figure,* she thought as they got into the Jeep. As she had that thought, she was shaking her head in silent disbelief; Danny noticed.

"What is it?"

Geri realized that she had been shaking her head and maybe even talking to herself.

"Oh nothing, I guess—just trying to make sense of it all. Let's find a restaurant."

Chapter 32

Following the Vermont trip, Danny was back in the police station. After gearing up, he headed for the Detective Division. He wasn't going to delay getting the information out that their murderer who was too injured to make it to court wasn't too injured to party it up in Vermont, safe and away from the prying eyes of Maidstone. *Screw him*, Danny thought, *friggin asshole.*

Danny knocked on Detective Lieutenant Snyder's door and asked if he had a moment. Snyder was really busy and in no mood to talk to this rookie. He couldn't tell him that he was in the middle of scheduling security for some Wall Street types that were on their way up for a conference. The security had nothing to do with the police department. It had everything to do with a nice, fat moonlighting check he would get from his off the books security company. *Now this kid wants to talk police work. What a pain in my ass*, he thought.

"Yah, come in, just for a minute; I'm in the middle of something that I have to get done."

"It won't even take a minute," said Danny. "I just wanted to tell you that on my days off I was up in Stowe. When I went into the Long Trail Inn, who is there at the bar sucking down Long Island Ice Teas with a hot babe on his arm but Brad Worthington. He's too injured to go to court, just not too injured to be out partying."

The Detective Lieutenant looked up, surprised and in disbelief.

"That dumb son-of–a-bitch. Thanks, I'll take care of this."

"Yes, sir" and Danny was out the door almost as soon as he had arrived.

Walking down the hallway Danny thought to himself, *"Yes, Worthington is a dumb-son-of-a-bitch."* As he repeated the statement several times to himself, he tried doing it in the Detective Lieutenant's voice and manner of speech. Each time Danny repeated the phrase, he got closer to saying it the way the Detective Lieutenant said it. Something isn't right, what did the Lieutenant really mean? Then the portable radio barked at him. It was back on the road for another call to respond to in quiet Maidstone, Massachusetts.

The night of the murder Danny had been instructed not to make out a report. He knew that at some point he would have to testify, so he started making more notes adding to the ones he had made at the scene. As time went on, he kept refining the notes until it was an actual report. It wasn't on a department form, it was unofficial. It was complete, detailed, accurate, done in chronological order, and still not an official report. A supervisor wouldn't review it and sign off on the contents. It wouldn't get filed in records. It was; a true accounting of what Danny had done that night. Supervising District Attorney Cohen had beaten it into the class that proper note taking, and report writing was essential to good police work and prosecution. The memory fades and people talk, especially police officers, and then the facts get changed.

"Write everything down," he would say. "And when you're done, read it over and over again and make sure it's right. Before you go to court, read your report. Now when you're done reading your report, and you think you're done,

159

read it again. It could be months or years before you testify. In court we need what you did that night, not how you remember it today."

Great advice, sound reasoning, the best of police practice was the theme that Supervising District Attorney Marvin Cohen would repeatedly pound into the officers who took his classes. So, with that in mind, it still bothered him that the Detective Lieutenant had told him not to write up a report. He didn't want conflicting information. *The facts were the facts, right?*

While in the process of putting all his information down in his unofficial report, he kept coming up with the same question: *how did Penny get a slug to the left rear side of her head and numb nuts have that damage to his left hand? Did the slug pass through his hand? The jaggedness of his injury that night didn't look like a hole; it just looked like an animal had bitten him and ripped a chunk of flesh off.* Danny knew that a high-powered slug gun did have a heck of a muzzle blast. He had always been careful not to be too close to one and to avoid firing if someone else was close to the muzzle. He still wasn't sure what the results would be to a person's skin. *Could the muzzle blast have caused that injury?*

Time to do some experiments, thought Danny. *Now I have to find someone who will let me borrow a 10-gauge shotgun. There aren't many guns that come in that size. First off, they kick like a mule; and for most bird hunting, they are just too big and destroy whatever you hit. Anyone using a 10-gauge would be shooting at Canada Geese high overhead or maybe a turkey at a great distance. The shotgun that night had been set up for deer hunting. Even with a target the size of a deer, a round that big would damage more meat and was considered over-kill.* Still there were a few out there, and Danny had to find one.

He asked around, and didn't tell anyone the real reason for needing that size shotgun. He made up a story that he was thinking of going deer hunting and wanted to try several shotguns before he dropped a bunch of money and ended up with a shotgun he didn't like. Being the Berkshires, there were any number of people with hunting rifles and shotguns. So not to tip his hand, he tried several of various sizes and calibers even though they were not the specific model and caliber/gauge he was looking for. In those offered, there was only one 10-gauge shotgun that was similar to what he needed for comparison. Numerous people were more than happy to display their rifles and shotguns. They were proud of their purchases and wanting to show off their prized possession. Getting to be alone with the particular shotgun and fire it was a problem. He was only looking for one shotgun, that being the Browning 10-gauge. All the others he could fire with the owners because he wouldn't be doing any special testing. Danny was good with the rifles and shotguns, so good that he fired most of them more accurately and consistently than the people who owned them. He even ended up giving instructions to the various owners to improve their personal shooting skills. The problem was he had to be alone with the Browning. He had found several rifles and even a shotgun that had just about the same barrel length and the same distance back to the trigger. That part of his theory proved itself that Penny could not have done anything to fire the weapon and that Brad had to be holding the shotgun in a most awkward position. It also showed that he really wanted to shoot Penny and that the killing was no accident. Penny could have grabbed the barrel; still Brad had to pull the trigger. He held her pinned against the wall, and only he could've really directed the muzzle into her head. Even in the strangest of circumstances if she had pulled the muzzle to her head, it was

Brad's finger on the trigger. It was Brad's hand that had to be aligned with the muzzle in such close proximity that the blast tore into it. Those positions drew a picture of a young lady, forced up against the wall with Brad's left hand when the trigger was pulled.

One gun owner had enough rifles and shotguns to outfit a good size platoon; and in the mix he had a 10-gauge Browning shotgun. Danny had fired them all, and the 10-gauge kicked the hell out of him. There was a tremendous blast from the muzzle. Danny wanted to be able to measure and document the damage it could cause. The gun owner loved sharing his rifles and shotguns with Danny and learned a thing or two about shooting from Danny, the expert. That was when the plan came together. Danny knew that the owner had to head to the airport to catch a flight. So, he timed his arrival at the house to ask a favor to fire the 10-gauge one last time before he decided to buy. Danny knocked on the door; and when the owner opened it, Danny could see that the suitcases were right there just inside the door ready to go.

"Oh," stated Danny, "I forgot you were heading out today."

"Yah, I have to leave in ten minutes, or I will miss my flight. I'm meeting up with the wife in Hilton Head. Great golfing if you like golf. You just have to watch out for the alligators in the water hazards."

"Oh shoot," said Danny in as disappointing a voice as he could muster.

"Why, what's the problem?" the owner asked.

"I was hoping to fire the 10-gauge one last time just too make sure it was right for me. I see you're heading out so maybe when you get back."

"That won't be for three weeks, will that work for you?"

"Bummer," said Danny. "That will be two weeks to late. I guess I will just have to wing it." Danny had laid the path for the owner, and now he held his breath to see if the owner would take the bait.

The owner was busy moving his belongings to the car, and Danny was helping when the owner finally came to the option Danny was hoping for.

"How about I let you take the shotgun, and you can fire it when you get the chance. I am not going to need it at Hilton Head, and you can lock it up in the police station until I get back. How does that sound?"

"Perfect," said Danny, "just perfect." The owner had no idea that he had just been set up. He liked Danny and trusted him so how big a deal was loaning a police officer a shotgun? Besides, it was always nice to have a police officer owe you a favor.

"That sounds great," Said Danny, "and I will swing by the house and check on things if you like."

Perfect, the owner thought, *I am already getting a return on my favor.*

Shotgun in hand, Danny headed back to the station; and the owner was on his way to Hilton Head. Both thought they were way ahead of the game. The owner now had free private security on his place, and Danny had his test example.

Chapter 33

Unfortunately for Danny, he was now one more step closer to finding answers to questions that just might get him killed. He was trying to solve one riddle. His actions were causing things to come into line that he could never have imagined. If someone had told him the direction this was going to take beforehand, he would have never have believed them. It would have been like someone describing what was going to happen on September 11, 2001, the day before, and expecting people to believe that those year-long sequence of events could actually have happened. If some spook from the CIA had gone to Congress or the President on September 10th and laid it out without the names just the plan that they had uncovered, he would have been dismissed as a crazy conspiracy theorist. On September 10, 2001, no one would ever believe that nineteen men, armed with box cutters, could hijack four planes at the same time and slam them into buildings in New York and Washington D. C., but it happened. Danny was setting things in motion far beyond Brad Worthington and Maidstone, Massachusetts.

Danny went to the local gun shop and picked up several boxes of 10-gauge slug ammo. Some had rounded heads, and some had pointed tips. He remembered that when they were processing the scene that there had been pieces of lead chunks in the room. He couldn't tell if it were a round nosed or pointed, so he got both. As Danny headed out the door, the gun shop owner wished him luck and hoped he would get his deer.

Danny thanked him and promised that he'd do his best to bag at least one. The owner didn't know he was hoping to bag a murderer, not a deer. Danny thought about deer hunting, and while he had eaten venison before and liked it, he couldn't bring himself to shoot a one. Shooting some people would be easy, a deer not so much. Deer are delicious; unfortunately you have to kill them to have one for dinner. They are just too harmless a creature for Danny to be blowing one away. Danny had fired his rifle at people numerous times over the years. He never once regretted firing, unlike TV, he wasn't sure if he ever hit anything he told himself. He sincerely hoped he had. In a real gun battle, you're ducking as much as firing. When your target is 300 yards away and six people are cranking off rounds at the insurgent, everyone wants a piece of him. So, if you move forward and by chance find a body with holes in it, no one knows for sure who connected and who didn't. For Danny, if he missed it wasn't for lack of trying. As for the deer, if someone offered him a venison steak he would take it. If he had to get a piece of meat, he would go to the local grocery store or a restaurant.

Danny stopped by the town hall and picked up several phone books that had been left for recycling. These weren't real test dummies. They were free and would be a good start. Danny headed for the local sand pit to start the experiment.

Remembering Supervising District Attorney Cohens advice, he started making notes. Which type of round did he fire? What was the distance to the target? What was the point of impact? He made sure to take the before and after photographs, documenting everything. He had never done this before as a police officer. He relied on the classes he had

165

taken and every TV crime episode that he could think of. The people on crime shows might be an actress or an actor, but those shows did have expert technical advisors on staff to call on so that they followed proper procedure. Danny had to do this now; he couldn't wait until he had a degree in forensic science.

The first rounds were fired at six inches into the center of the phonebooks. They left a huge burn pattern on the cover and punched a massive hole straight through. The burn pattern showed a circle and stippling from the unburned powder as it impacted the cover.

Danny then fired at the edge of the phone book from two feet away so that the round made contact with just the edge ever so slightly. Again, there was the burn pattern on the cover and some heavy stippling with the clean partial hole from front to back. The edges of the pages were somewhat torn up and showed some damage. Danny kept making notes and changing books to get a clean, fresh idea of everything that was happening.

He set up the next test, and this time the muzzle was right at the edge of the cover, and the slug travelled down the side of the phone book, front to back without striking the phone book. When the shotgun fired, even Danny jumped from the blast. It tore into the pages of the phone book, shredding them into tiny pieces of confetti. The book itself went sailing off, tumbling about six feet away. The edge of the book showed a jagged half circle path of destruction.

Danny examined the book; and then shaking his head pronounced to no one, *It was the muzzle blast; damn that is powerful. It most certainly did the damage to Brad that I saw that night.*

Danny was packing things up and cleaning up the area not wanting to leave a mess or any indication of what he had been up to. The phone books were history. He could drop them off at the recycling center, where no one would see them. As he headed back to town, he realized that he still had one more test to do. *I need to do this on something that more closely resembles a person's hand. The phone books definitely show that it's possible, now to invest in a fresh chicken.*

Danny was back at the sand pit, and the muzzle blast from the shotgun sent the chicken sailing off into the dirt shredded like a wild animal had torn it apart. Danny had proved to himself how Brad had gotten the nasty rip in his hand. He also had to clean chicken parts off of himself and the $2,000 slug gun he had borrowed. The blast did rip into Brad's hand. That would have certainly resulted in the jagged wound he had seen the night of the murder. He had only a slight glimpse of Brad's injury. It was so jagged and painful looking that, like Penny lying in the bedroom, the images were burned into his mind. Too bad he couldn't download those images and print them out. He would also like to hit the delete key to his brain, that wasn't happening either.

Now I know, Danny thought. *The guys at the forensic lab must have figured this out a long time ago. I wish I could have seen their report. It would have saved a lot of time and not made such a mess. Anything having to do with this case was kept under lock and key with a strict need to know.* Danny thought this was still open-and-shut case with the limited number of people involved as in the victim and the murderer. Then there was the very short time span between the report of the shooting and the officers arriving on scene. There were the repeated statements to the Dispatcher, and moments later the same statement Brad made to the first responding officers. *Who were they keeping the information from? Why all the secrecy? It wasn't like they had developed an informant that the department would be worried about disclosing. Sometime before the trial, the District*

167

Attorney's Office would have to disclose all the evidence they had to the defense team, so they were going to find out about it anyway. In general terms, everyone in town knew what had happened, so what gives? Why the secrecy?

Was someone actively trying to protect Brad and if so, who? Was the department giving orders or taking them? Being so far down the food chain in the department and the town, it wasn't his place to ask, maybe he should have.

Well, now I know and, I am sure the forensic lab guys know. I have a few more dots to connect; I think I already have the answer. Like the chicken test, I want to know for sure. I am going to need some help.

Chapter 34

Danny made a phone call.

"Hey, Geri, how's it goin?"

Geri was a little surprised and glad to hear his voice in an up-beat tone. "All things considered, fine. What's up?"

"Would you be interested in holding a gun on someone?"

"I guess I could do that. Is there anyone in particular?"

"Yes, that would be me."

"Now what have you done that you need a State Trooper to hold a gun on you? You didn't go after Worthington, did you? If you did, don't say another word on the phone."

Danny laughed. "Why yes, I am going after numb-nuts, just not that way; and, no, I am not going to get arrested or charged with stalking or anything else. I have an idea, and it takes two people. One subject needs to be about your height and have a similar arm length."

"At this time, I will give a qualified yes. I reserve the right to back out if this gets just a tad weird."

"It will get a tad weird because if it doesn't, then my theory is wrong, and I am back to square one. I could explain it over the phone, showing you would be much less confusing and easier to understand. Plus, if you show up and play your cards right, I might buy you dinner."

"What are my chances for a back rub?"

"Nearly perfect."

"No deal."

"Okay, okay, back rub guarantied, only after dinner."

"I'll be there, what time?"

Geri was ready for another back rub, and Danny was ready to see if he was right. The back rub would just be an added bonus. *Back rubs and running water, who knew?*

Geri showed up right on time, and Danny could not hide his excitement. She was thrilled to see such a positive response until she realized it was more about testing the theory than seeing her again. She was only partly right, at this point, the fact that Danny was glad she was there wasn't showing.

"OK," Danny announced, "we need to go into the bedroom."

"Slow down, big boy. You think you can call up anytime you want, and 60 seconds after I show up, we're bumping uglies?"

Danny realized the way it sounded and tried to correct himself. "No, it's part of the theory I am trying to test."

"What is your theory, that female State Troopers are easy?"

"No, no, no. Please sit down, and I'll explain."

"What, now you want to do it on the couch?"

In hopes that things could not get worse, Danny blurted out, "I think I know for sure how Brad killed Penny."

Now that got Geri's attention, she couldn't help one last jab. "So, the back rub is out?"

"Not a chance, but that's later."

"Good, I like a positive attitude. So, what's your theory and what does a bedroom have to do with it?"

Danny took a deep breath trying to prepare for a long, detailed explanation of the facts and physical evidence as he knew it. Once more Danny had to put himself back in that bedroom and make sense of something that no matter how you spun it would never make sense. It didn't have to be a bedroom, but he wanted to recreate everything the way it was that night.

"First off, most rounds fired from a 10-gauge slug gun will travel in a straight line until they hit something very hard or thick. Even when they hit a deer or a person, they tend to go straight through. There isn't much that will cause the round to deflect MOST of the time. The shape of the bullet, the weight, and the speed just push it straight through almost anything."

Geri was not a ballistics expert. She did have some experience firing shotguns, though nothing of this size. Knowing that this was bigger than the 12-gauge shotguns she was familiar with, she agreed with that statement and nodded her head.

Danny continued. "If that's the case, then all you have to do is line up the objects that the slug penetrated to form a straight line. Most of the objects collected that night have just a round hole and not a jagged tear from a fragment."

Geri thought about the first statement and then the second putting the two together. After a moment she again nodded her head in agreement that both actions sounded possible.

"OK, so here are the objects we know were somehow impacted by the slug. First, we have the start point, the muzzle of the shotgun."

Geri nodded once more thinking of the massive chunk of lead exploding from the barrel of the shotgun.

"Next," Danny said, "we have the slug impacting the left rear side of Penny's head entering above and just behind the left ear and exiting the back of her skull. I wasn't present at the autopsy, so I can't say that for a fact. That's what it looked like to me."

"Ok, let's go with that for now. What else?"

"Now the slug enters the wall a little under 5 feet off the floor and on a slight up angle.. The hole is bigger than the slug diameter. Some of the skull, brains and a long wad of her hair are imbedded in the wall making the opening bigger."

The last details struck Geri like a ton of bricks. She knew bullets and slugs could do such things, fortunately for her had she never seen it in real life. She could only imagine what was going through Danny's mind that night and now re-telling the incident about two people he knew personally. She could see Danny was in full cop mode looking only for the facts and not reliving it the way he did when he first told her about the murder when they were up in Stowe.

With a shudder she nodded her head again and added, "I follow you so far. Did the slug exit the wall?"

"Yes, and it went out much larger in diameter than it went in. The sheetrock, insulation and plywood trapped a lot of the softer material; the hair, skull, and brains. When it came out, it went sailing off into the woods. The hole in the wall was not quite level with the floor, and there was just a slight angle to the trajectory."

"So, the shotgun had to be pointed almost straight on?" stated Geri.

"Just about, hang on, there's more. Most of the brains, skull, and other material were splattered on the wall behind Penny. The blood and skull splattered the wall and fell on the floor or went in other directions bouncing off. Where she was pressed up against the wall there is a protected area that her body and the sheet had covered. There is the smear on the wall where she slid down when she collapsed. Of course, Brad let go of her as soon as the blast tore his hand apart."

Geri could see that re-telling the incident was starting to get to him. His voice was starting to reveal emotion, and his hands were shaking just enough so that she could notice.

He continued on. "We now have one more item to put into the trajectory, and that is Brad's hand."

Geri had been concentrating on everything else and had forgotten about the hand. Danny had told her all about it when they were up in Stowe. That injury rated Brad a trip to the emergency room and not the police station. Of course, his new love interest had taken care of him in his time of need after his wife's tragic death.

Danny pulled out pictures of the phone book starting with the straight on shots that penetrated the books and the ring they made around the clean hole. He then showed the pictures of the phone books with the grazing shot and the damage it had done. Then he pulled out the photo of the book where he had held the muzzle next to the side of the book and the way it had torn the pages open.

Geri was surprised at the damage done to the book by the muzzle blast and was looking at it closely. She made the comment that the blast would make a nasty wound. Then Danny pulled out one last picture.

"What the hell is that? That's not a part of a person is it?"

"No, that's what happens to a chicken from the muzzle blast. The barrel was just about touching, and it did that kind of damage."

"Damn," was all she could say as she stared at the picture. Geri kept going over the pictures and reviewing the theory.

173

"So what do you want me to do?"

"First off, I want to try and line up all of the objects and get an actual picture of it to prove my theory."

"That is going to be real creepy. Okay, if you think it will help. Why am I holding the gun and not you? You're a guy, he's a guy, and a he shot her."

"True enough; you saw him at the bar, he's about as tall as you are. My arms are much longer than his arms. Size wise you are closer to his size than I am; and for the demo, that's important."

Geri agreed. She wasn't happy with the idea, still she agreed. They entered the bedroom, and the shotgun was there on the bed

"Oh, shit, this is really creepy," she said staring at the shotgun.

"Don't worry. It's unloaded, and the bolt is to the rear and the chamber is open and empty. It can't be fired. Please, check it out."

Geri walked over to the bed, and without touching the shotgun, she closely examined it. The safety was on. Yes, the bolt was to the rear and a slug could not be fired from it. While knowing that, it was still creeping her out. She reached down and rechecked the shotgun once more. "Ok, now what?" Before Danny could speak, she pointed the shotgun away from Danny and inserted her pinky finger into the chamber to make sure it was empty. Geri lifted the shotgun up knowing that the bolt was to the rear and that her finger had confirmed that there wasn't a round in the chamber. She then pointed the shotgun at the light coming in from the window and looked down through the barrel to confirm that there was light coming through. Now she was absolutely sure that nothing was in there.

"Okay, now what?" she asked.

174

"Let's start lining things up. Put your right hand and index finger in the area of the trigger. Now place the muzzle right next to your left hand."

Geri extended her left arm and pulled back her right arm to give her enough distance so that the muzzle touched her hand. She was now in a stance like she was holding a bow and arrow and was drawing back on the string to launch an arrow. It was a very awkward pose trying to get the distance between having her finger on the trigger and getting the muzzle to be next to her left hand.

"Now the last piece of the puzzle," and Danny put his head up against the wall so that the left side was exposed. He had placed a piece of tape at the five-foot level and positioned his head next to it. "Come over to me with the shotgun to get the angle." Danny had to get his head firmly against the wall so that Geri could get up to him for the right trajectory. "Put your left hand across my face with your thumb near my ear. Hold that a second."

Danny tried to reach the trigger from his position, even with his much longer arm; he couldn't get anywhere close to the trigger.

Geri stared at Danny, checked all the positions, and tried to think of some other way things could have happened. She lowered the shotgun and stepped back.

"The son-of-a-bitch pinned her to the wall and blew her brains out," was all Geri could say.

All Danny could manage to say was a weak almost unheard, "Yes." In a soft voice of a resigned and frustrated man, Danny asked Geri to hang in there while he set up the camera on a tripod, so they could take some photos using the timer on the camera. He had found the answer he was looking for and was saddened by the fact that he was right. He was right about what happened, and still frustrated because he still couldn't understand any of it.

They took several photos from different angles just to confirm the theory. As they were wrapping things up, Danny questioned himself. *Why am I doing this? The forensic guys will have all this, and they are the experts. I guess just had to prove it to myself, to see it for a certainty, to know for a fact what really happened. That way, when I get to court I will know beyond a shadow of a doubt that Brad killed her, not by accident or that she had any hand in this. This was a murder, plain and simple.*

As they headed down to the Butternut Brewery, Bear, sensing food, joined them.

"Ya know, Danny, you really know how to show a girl a good time."

Danny realized too late that he had probably screwed things up beyond repair.

"If you don't want to go, I understand."

"Oh no, big boy, we're going. You're buying, and I am getting the most expensive thing on the menu."

"A last meal is it?"

"Next time," said Geri, "if there is a next time, it better be a little more romantic than re-creating a murder scene if you catch my drift."

One more second chance, thought Danny; *don't screw it up.*

Geri looked at the menu and was ready to scream. She held back and smiled sweetly at the waitress as she read off the specials. "We'll need a few minutes more," Geri said, and the waitress departed to see to another table.

"All three specials tonight are chicken, is this set up? You show me pictures of a blown-up chicken, and then this?"

There goes my last second chance. "Hey, you picked the place not me. I give up, I can't win."

"Oh, you're a winner all right. If it weren't for Bear, I would've been outta here a long time ago. I love your dog. You I can tolerate, but it's wearing thin."

"Bear is a great buddy. He makes up for a lot of my short comings, and he is much more handsome. The downside is that he always tries to cut in. So, if I keep Bear I might get to see you again?"

Geri really liked this nut case Jarhead, even though she wasn't sure why. Yes, she liked Bear, now if Danny were a jerk, then Bear wouldn't have been able to help. Chances are she wouldn't have liked Bear either. The dog and their masters generally share a lot of personality traits. An easy-going dog usually means an easy-going master, and a hyper dog will have a whacked-out owner. Yippee dogs/yippee owners. Bear loves to cuddle. Could this guy really be a Marine that likes to cuddle? He could reasonably be successfully doing other things, back rubs included when he puts his mind to it.

"Did any of your teachers ever note on your report card that you didn't apply yourself?" asked Geri.

"Just about all of them," said Danny, "just about all of them. Did you get a peek at my high school record? What the hell brought that up?"

"No, can't say that I've seen your record. How are you doing in college?"

"A bunch of As and one B in sociology. The professor doesn't like cops and hates Marines."

"Well, it sounds like you are applying yourself now. Take a lesson from Bear, go easy on yourself. You'll last a lot longer and meet more chicks."

"I'm having enough trouble with one right now. Why would I want to add to my frustration meeting more chicks?"

Danny looked across the table at the grinning State Trooper. "I am doing just fine as I am, thank you very much," he said.

Yes, you are big boy; yes, you are, and don't screw this up, thought Geri.

All Danny got was a sneaky devilish smile in response.

"Now what," he wanted to know.

"Oh nothing."

Meaning something, he knew. Anytime a woman says, "Oh nothing" then it really means something and usually something big.

"Let's order, my back hurts."

I don't see how this is still working, thought Danny. *She is hungry and still wants a back rub after all this. I don't understand it. I can't explain it; somehow it's still working so I guess I will go with the flow.* He looked across the table and couldn't help thinking how soft and nice her back felt when he touched it. The equally soft blues eyes made up for the touch of an attitude he frequently encountered.

Chapter 35

Danny was back in Court for Brad's next date. It came and went in less than a minute. "A continuance is requested by the Defense. No objection from the Prosecution."

"Case continued," ordered the Judge.

Danny was dumb founded and walked out shaking his head. Confused, he kept saying to himself that this was unbelievable. He reminded himself that he had told the Detective Lieutenant about Brad's partying in Vermont; *they can't still be buying his injury bullshit.* Yet here we are waiting for a new court date. *This sucks.*

Now, even more time passed, and nothing was happening with the court case. Danny had gone over his notes, his unofficial report, the sketch, and now the photos of the re-enactment dozens of times. He wanted to make sure he was prepared. Marvin Cohen had stressed this when preparing to testify. There was no such thing as being over prepared when it came to testifying and the dreaded cross examination. More cops got screwed up not by doing a good job, but by not being prepared for the cross examination. A defense attorney didn't care how nice you are or how professional you acted. All he wanted to do was to tear your testimony to pieces and leave what is legally called a reasonable doubt in the minds of the jury. The District Attorney would go over your case. Most of the time, he wasn't going to try to discredit your testimony while he was preparing you to testify. Tear yourself apart long before you testify and make the corrections you need. Tell the truth and only the truth and be prepared to be called a liar, an idiot, and a bumbling misguided fool. Know that this negative attack will be coming and be ready. Be on guard, and always and forever, tell the truth. A bad truth is much better than any good lie. One lie, one attempt to deviate from the truth, and you can blow the case and maybe even your job. Cops that are caught lying get fired. Defense attorneys that are caught lying are considered to being doing their job.

Marvin Cohen, Supervising District Attorney, was a prick with a capital "P," and he was right. One lie; one exaggeration, one embellishment, one off-the-cuff editorializing could sink critical testimony and let a perpetrator go. Not in his court room, not if he could help it.

And then it happened; Danny arrived at the police station for the afternoon shift. He had collected his gear from his locker and was ready to hit the break room for a coffee and to find out what had been going on the past twenty-four hours. He was reading some computer printouts when the Dispatcher announced, "It's over."

"That's nice," said Danny, half paying attention. He kept on walking and reading.

"No dude, it's really over," the Dispatcher stated, this time in a much louder voice.

The tone and volume stopped Danny, he still had no idea what the Dispatcher was talking about.

Danny turned now, curious and asked, "OK, what's happening that's now over?" Danny wondered if he had missed some interesting call in the past twenty-four hours. He hadn't seen anything in the printouts or on the board.

"The case against Worthington is over," the Dispatcher almost shouted.

Danny stopped in his tracks. *Holy shit, I didn't even have to testify. He must have rolled over and took the deal. He probably knew we had him especially after I saw him playing footsie with his shrink drinking booze when he was too injured and medicated to be in court. Finally, his BS caught up to him, and he's going away. Chances are that he will never see his Playboy Model shrink again.* Yes! How much time did the little bastard get?"

"Get?" said the Dispatcher. "He didn't get shit. The District Attorney accepted a plea of negligent homicide, and he got seven years' probation and 250 hours of community service."

Danny at first thought he was joking. The look on the Dispatcher's face confirmed his worst fear. *That little, mean, rich punk of an asshole had just gotten away with murder.*

Danny didn't think he could get more enraged until he saw the newspapers detailing the case and the sentence of seven years' probation.

The Supervising District Attorney for Berkshire County was quoted as saying, "After hearing all the evidence and wanting to spare Penelope Worthington's family anymore pain that an agreed sentence had been reached with the defendant. In that the defendant had admitted to his crime and his involvement in open court and that based on the evidence and the defendant's extreme remorse for his actions, the District Attorney's Office has agreed to the plea deal and hopes that as the grief passes; everyone will be able to move on in the future."

Danny was shouting out loud to no one. He was yelling at the trees and the swamps and the hills. Here was the toughest, strictest, most by the book District Attorney; and he was letting a murderer get off with probation. How could a man who held police officers and other attorneys up to such high standards of justice and professionalism roll over and let this guy walk. Cohen had been one of the most respected, honorable, and dedicated people Danny had ever met and now this. There was no justice for Penny in this outcome, and now real grief was hitting Danny. He did his part, and now he was a part of a massive failure.

Then there was the phone call from Geri.

"What the hell happened?" a surprised and confused Geri wanted to know. "How could this guy get probation? Seven years sounds like a long time for probation, but he should have been doing twenty to life. Did you get the facts wrong?" she asked.

Danny was already taking this personally. Now with Geri's implied accusation, it cut to the quick. In slow, deliberate, halting words Danny responded, "No, I got it right, and Mr. Cohen has a lot of explaining to do. I have a class with him in two days, and I intend to have a little chat with him. It may cost me my job, at this point I don't care. I am ready to bag the whole thing and get off to Forestry School and put cops and robbers behind me if shit like this is going to happen."

Danny wasn't paying any attention to who was nearby while he vented on the phone. He should have found a more private space than the roll call room at the police station, but that was where he was when Geri called. She was demanding answers, answers that he wanted, too. An officer passing by could hear the exchange, and it echoed down the hall where anyone could hear, anyone.

Geri had hit a nerve and hit it harder than she had thought. She could not conceal her surprise or outrage at the verdict, and she didn't blame Danny. How on earth did the

District Attorney come to that agreed sentence, she wanted to know.

"Danny, I know it wasn't you, just how is this possible?"

"I don't know, I will find out," and he hung up.

The police station was as quiet as Main Street at 2am on a Sunday morning. The last statement was not shouted. It didn't have to be. It could've been heard anywhere on the floor. When the conversation started, everyone within ear shot stopped talking and they hung on every word. Danny wanted answers and by the tone of his voice and his choice of words, it was obvious that he was going to get them. He would get them no matter where this took him or who he pissed off along the way. When a Marine is given an assignment, he completes the assignment successfully. If he isn't successful, then he keeps at it until he is. There is no middle ground. There is *no, I got most of it done.* Failure is never an option.

Geri looked at the humming phone and slowly punched the off button to silence the noise. She thought back to that night in Stowe and the chance encounter at the Long Trail Inn. She hoped Danny could find a sturdy steering wheel somewhere. If he didn't, someone was going to get hurt, and Danny was going to be in big trouble.

Chapter 36

Danny didn't find a steering wheel, he did grab Bear. With a light pack, some snacks, and water, he headed out to the Appalachian Trail near Butternut and started walking, and walking, and walking. Finally, Bear had had enough and just laid down on the trail refusing to move. Danny was about to go Marine Corps on Bear. Quickly he realized that Bear had nothing to do with this and it would be totally wrong to take it out on him. Instead he plopped down next to Bear, and they shared the snacks and the water and eventually dozed off. During the entire hike, Danny had been running through his mind every detail he knew about the case. He was trying to figure out what had gone wrong. He tried to pick holes in the case looking at it from the other side. Danny was not a seasoned investigator; then again the facts are facts. Even a less experienced officer could see the truth. With all his second guessing and nit-picking, it was still coming up murder. He couldn't wait to hear Supervising District Attorney Cohen's explanation for this outcome. If the most senior law enforcement official in Berkshire County had just thrown a murder case, then he was going to find out why. This had to be a bag job pure and simple. The night of the murder everything had been done by the book as far as Danny could tell. He didn't see where they'd made any mistakes. Between the multiple confessions and the physical evidence, a conviction for murder should have been a slam dunk. Seven years' probation was outrageous.

Danny was going to ask Cohen directly with no beating around the bush. He would find out why, and then what? Who would he go to for help? He was already at the top of the local law enforcement chain with Attorney Cohen. Who could he go to?

First things first, thought Danny. *I will find out why and then figure out where to go. No sense getting too far ahead until I know the facts.*

Bear and Danny headed down the mountain and back to the barn. He had a lot to do to prepare for his encounter with Mr. Cohen. Danny was going to be as organized and prepared as though he was going to court because in his mind he was. Supervising District Attorney Cohen was known for verbally destroying police officers who screwed up cases and Danny didn't want to be one of them. He also knew that one wrong step on his part would result in one hundred verbal razor blade cuts that he would never survive. He went over each and every detail, speaking out loud, with Bear as his audience. Bear listened, tracking him with his eyes as he moved about the apartment making his case. Then, the final question: *How could this mutt get probation for murder?* After several rounds of this, Danny decided he was ready and waited for class to begin.

Chapter 37

As Danny walked into class that night, Supervising District Attorney Cohen locked eyes with him. He hadn't said a word; and this guy is looking at him with a piercing, questioning look. Without blinking or looking away, he just returned the stare, no greeting, no acknowledgment.

Danny didn't hear a word of the lecture, and Cohen also seemed to be distracted. Normally his lectures came out like a machinegun firing bursts of sentences. They would come out so fast that no one had time to do anything else except concentrate on what he was saying. Now he was stumbling, losing track of his thoughts, jumping around and talking in fragmented sentences. Danny barely noticed. He was concentrating on his thoughts and could care less what Cohen was saying because after this night he was never coming back to class. *I don't need to listen to this asshole one more night with his high and mighty bullshit that he decides is mandatory for everyone else except him.*

Attorney Cohen's classes always went right down to the last minute. Tonight he ended the lecture a half hour early. The entire class was surprised. They were not going to question getting out early. They made a break for the door and a quick exit. That is everyone except for Danny. He stayed seated until almost everyone had left the room and then slowly rose taking a stance that could only be described as

Marine Corps defiant. District Attorney Cohen also took a stance facing Danny. He made no attempt to gather up his books or notes and made no request for Danny to leave. He just stood, his eyes locked on Danny's.

Cohen was the first to speak, and it was in total character with his historical persona.

"Why in the world did your department process the crime scene and not call in the State Police Major Case Squad?" Danny wasn't ready for that question or any other questions. He thought that he would be the one asking the questions.

"I have no idea, as a rookie patrolman they don't consult with me on those matters." The response came off way too condescending and arrogant for a student to be talking to a Professor of Marvin Cohen's stature.

"Why did you give murderer probation?" Danny countered.

Having his judgement and actions questioned by a student and a rookie patrolman was not something Attorney Cohen was used to. Anyone who did question him rarely survived the encounter with his pride and dignity intact. District Attorney Cohen's whole life revolved around words and being quick; and he was a master. Few ever made it to that level.

"Getting into a domestic and trying to keep your wife from committing suicide is not murder, its manslaughter. When Penelope's family heard the facts, they just wanted things to go away and not cause any more pain. She was running around and got caught. He confronted her, and she went for the gun. He tried to stop her, and the gun went off accidently. Even manslaughter would have been tough to prove."

District Attorney Cohen and Danny were locked eyeball to eyeball during the entire brief exchange. In that brief time Attorney Cohen could see the look of confidence and defiance drain from Danny's face. The standing tall Marine was wilting before him. Danny's brain was moving at lightning speed. His voice could not come close to catching up. His mind was asking one hundred questions all at once, not a word could reach his lips. With no words coming from Danny, District Attorney Cohen collected his materials, placed them in a canvas tote, and headed for the door. As he made it to the door as almost an afterthought he turned and stated; "That was the most unprofessional processing of a crime scene I have ever had to deal with."

This was the first time Danny had ever heard about a suicide attempt or that Penny was the one to get the shotgun. They were both screwing around, not just her. *Where is this coming from*, Danny wondered?

He finally found his voice, but could only find a few words, "What about the confessions sir?"

Supervising District Attorney Cohen froze in his tracks like he had hit a concrete wall.

"What confession? There wasn't any confession."

Danny began to regain his composure. He never expected to hear about suicide and manslaughter. When he did, he tried to make it fit the scene that he had helped process. It didn't fit. While he was going through it in his head, he couldn't talk. Now the words were beginning to form a sentence.

"Not a confession," stated Danny, "confessions, like four or more confessions at two different times."

He now had Attorney Cohen's undivided attention. He put his bag down and backed up to sit on the top of the desk.

Crossing his arms in somewhat of a skeptical pose, he told Danny to go ahead.

Danny, having first prepared himself for the trial and then for this confrontation, began a slow, methodical monologue about that night and his part in it. His voice sounded more like a recording than a person having a conversation. Attorney Cohen did not once interrupt. He listened so intently that he did not hear the high winds thundering outside.

Danny began his recollection of that night with everyone standing near the control center, and the call coming in, "My wife is dead, I shot her." The dispatcher, not believing what he was hearing, repeated it back to the caller who made the same statement three times. Then the response to the house, and Danny and the first officer found Brad in the area of the driveway. Again, when asked what happened, Brad repeated," My wife is dead, I shot her." This time adding, "She is in the upstairs bedroom dead."

The monologue went on for close to 30 minutes without interruption. There was no emotion in Danny's voice— just a repeating of the facts as he knew them. Facts that he had practiced with Bear repeatedly to make sure he got them right. Danny even explained his re-creation of the shooting, how he lined up of the objects to show the straight line the massive slug took. In the end Danny was exhausted. His voice was a hoarse whisper coming from a dry throat. District Attorney Cohen was shocked, and utterly confused. This was something that never happened to him, until now.

Attorney Cohen reviewed what he had just heard from this young officer. He couldn't believe it or take it on face value. Did this officer actually see and hear these words? Or did he get this from someone else and was just passing it along.

He looked Danny straight in the eye and said, "I have gone over all the reports; I didn't see that you wrote one up. The only time you are mentioned is that you secured the house. If you were securing the outside of the house, how is it that you know about what happened inside? Plus, there was never any mention of a confession, much less repeated confessions."

Danny took it slow not wanting to make any errors in his words. If he screwed this up, he could be written off as a liar and never be trusted again.

"I didn't make out a report because I was told not to. The reason I was given was that the detectives only wanted one report so there wouldn't be any confusing or conflicting information."

"I did secure the house. My post was inside the bedroom where Penny had been murdered. I was also the second officer on scene. I went through the door right behind the first officer and into the bedroom. I was there from the start until almost the very end. I collected every piece of evidence except those items seized in the last half hour or so.

"I was there in dispatch and heard the conversation just a few feet away from the dispatcher along with three or more officers."

"I was there when we asked Brad what happened. I heard it all first hand. Didn't you get a download of the phone and radio transmissions that night to review as evidence?"

Now it was District Attorney Cohen's turn to look beaten.

"They told me that the electronic media had been destroyed in a lightning strike and wasn't available. There was no mention of his spontaneous utterance at the house. I didn't see a report from the other officer with you, and your name doesn't appear on any of the evidence tags, how's that?"

Danny began. "The scene was marked with evidence plaques and photographed in general showing the overall scene. Then each item seized was photographed with the numbered plaque in the photo. After each photo was taken, the detective taking the photo would look at the image on his screen to make sure it was what he wanted. If it wasn't, he would shoot it again until he got it right. He checked each and every shot. At that point, I would take an evidence bag and retrieve the item, seal the bag, and then a second detective would make the proper notes regarding each and every piece of evidence. This went on for hours. By the time I was told to leave the room we had seized over 150 separate items. When I left, there were still things that needed to be logged in."

"Each item was separately photographed?" Attorney Cohen asked.

"Yes, every damn one."

Attorney Cohen recalled the number of photos he had seen, and it was nowhere near 150.

"How many photos do you think were taken?" he asked.

Danny thought back, he wasn't the one taking the photos, so he could only guess.

Supervising District Attorney Cohen was going from shock and surprise to one very pissed-off individual. As mad as he was getting, he was still the District Attorney. He was going to get the facts and then heads would roll. He was going to have someone's ass for sure.

"Why wasn't the scene videoed?"

"It was, inside and out. The video covered everything the still photos did including zooming in and out on each numbered plaque and the item to be seized that was associated with each number."

"Son-of-a-bitch," was all that Cohen could say.

"Don't tell me," said Danny, "no video?"

Attorney Cohen shook his head very slowly. "I've been sandbagged."

Cohen was now thinking down the road. "Do you have any notes, photos, names?"

At this point Danny knew the case had been intentionally compromised. He still wasn't absolutely sure who was responsible. It could have been Attorney Cohen who was now playing a good role as a victim like Danny and Penny. He could be getting ready to cover his tracks. Danny had to take a chance, and at the same time cover his butt in case he was talking to a co-conspirator to cover-up a murder. There was only one way to find out and that was to keep moving forward.

"I don't have any photos of the scene. Like the report, I was told not to take any pictures. He searched my cell phone to make sure I didn't have any."

"Who's *he*?" asked Attorney Cohen.

"Detective Lieutenant Snyder."

At the same time Danny fished out a report and the demonstration photos he had taken and handed them over.

Chapter 38

District Attorney Cohen looked at the pages of the report and the photos and with a concerned look and asked Danny, "I thought you said you didn't make a report or have photos."

Now Cohen was wondering who was sandbagging him. Trust between the officer and the District Attorney was a very fragile and fluctuating thing at this point. Neither one trusted the other, both wanted answers.

An exasperated Danny shrugged and then informed Attorney Cohen that he had been told not to make an official report. He told Attorney Cohen he had made several pages of notes and a diagram of the scene that night while he waited for the detectives to arrive thinking that he would have to make a report later that evening. Days after the murder he decided to take his notes and turn it into a report for himself. He anticipated that somewhere down the road he would be called to testify. He wanted to get the facts straight and not forget anything. The demo photos were to prove to himself the way he thought the murder took place—did in fact take place. He wanted to prove that the death was a murder. The idea that this was a suicide never crossed his mind. He had only shared this information with one other person until tonight.

"Didn't the forensic people come up with the same information that I had? That she was pinned to the wall and shot in almost a straight on angle?" Danny asked.

"No," was the whispered response, "there wasn't any forensic report, just the medical examiner's report."

Another question popped into Attorney Cohen's head. "How can you be so sure that she didn't go after the shotgun to commit suicide and that there wasn't a struggle and the gun went off?"

"First off, when the shotgun fired, she couldn't reach the trigger and have the muzzle almost touching her head. Second, she would have had to be holding the shotgun almost straight out. Not likely. Third, why would she go find a shotgun and then come back to the bedroom and get under the covers naked with the shotgun to shoot herself?"

"How do you know she was naked and under the covers?" asked Attorney Cohen.

"It was in the photos. She was lying on the floor slumped against the wall. She was all twisted up in the sheet, blanket, and bed spread. She had to be under the covers, or she would have just slid off the wall and onto the floor. That had to be in the photos."

"The only photos of her body were of her lying off to the right side of bed on the floor, no clothes or bedding."

Danny racked his brain and then remembered. "We had untangled her body from the sheets and blanket at Lieutenant Snyder's direction. We then moved her over to the side so that the medical examiner could see the body and any other injuries. After checking the body, he then pronounced her dead. The M.E. didn't see her wrapped up in the sheets and blanket. He really didn't inspect the scene much—just a quick look around and some sad comments and left. He's a local M.E. and not a state forensic pathologist. He could pronounce people dead, and for the most part that is all he did."

"I have all the names of the officers and the dispatcher there in my report. It includes what they did, and the detectives assigned to the case that night. I'm not sure what went on outside the house or at the hospital. I don't have any information regarding the investigation that took place after I left the murder scene."

He explained how everything was kept secret, and only a select few in the detective unit might know about the interviews that were conducted over the period of several weeks.

As far as Penny cheating on Brad, the unconfirmed information that he had heard around town wasn't that she was cheating, it was that they were both swingers. Danny had been told that while swinging had been Brad's idea, Penny had been doing a lot better than he had. Penny was invited back more often, preferably without him. One of the rumors was that friends were buying Red Sox, Celtics, Bruins and Patriots tickets to give to Brad to get him out of town for the day or night or preferably the weekend. The district attorney had not heard about the psychiatrist in the E. R. the night of the murder. He was as surprised as Geri was to find out that Brad met his most recent girlfriend in the hospital. Cohen had no information about the trip to Stowe. Lieutenant Snyder never mentioned the fact that this injured, hurting person on pain killers was sucking down Long Island Ice Teas and was still standing and having a good ole time. Even Attorney Cohen could not believe that Brad had met his new love the night of the murder or the fact that she hadn't figured out what had gone down that night or maybe didn't care.

Questions and details kept going back and forth. This was cementing the facts and what could be proved and what couldn't. Those people who could be asked questions that wouldn't know that they were never mentioned in any reports and had important first-hand knowledge. District Attorney Cohen offered that he spoke almost exclusively with Detective Lieutenant Snyder about the case. He even told Danny that he had berated him for doing such a poor job of documentation. Lieutenant Snyder should have called the State Police Major Case Squad. There should've been a call to his office. They would have sent either a District Attorney or an investigator, or maybe both to the scene to coordinate efforts in the investigation. The Detective Lieutenant apologized all over the place and stated that from now on the State Police and the District Attorney's Office would always be called on every major case.

At the end of the day with the information that had been provided to his office by the Maidstone Police Detective Division, the only conclusion Supervising District Attorney Cohen's office could come up with was that it was a domestic with a suicide attempt. This action resulted in an accidental discharge that had caused Penny's death.

After several hours, the two parted. Cohen cautioned Danny not to speak to anyone about the case or of their conversation. Several people had seen Danny stay behind; no one knew what was said. At least they didn't think so. Danny had already voiced his opinion about the District Attorney's Office dropping the ball and screwing up the case. Danny apologized to Cohen for bad mouthing him.

"No, keep up that kind of talk," said Attorney Cohen. "If anyone asks or if it comes up in conversation, tell them that you are dropping out of class as soon as you can figure out how to do it without losing credit or funding. Be a jerk in class just not too big a pain in the ass, as no one would believe I would let that slide for long. Above all, let me get somethings moving on my end."

"Got it," was all Danny said. He was now focused, mad as hell, and totally focused.

"Of the paperwork that you have, what are you able to give to me tonight?"

"All of it," said Danny. "These are copies. I have the originals at home and also saved on the computer."

"What about the sketch?"

"You have a copy; I have a copy and the original, and have it scanned into my computer."

"Perfect," was the only reply.

That kind of pronouncement from Supervisory District Attorney Cohen was almost never heard.

Danny was hoping that he was putting his trust in the right person. If he got this wrong, then he was handing over everything to his enemy. This could be the person who bagged the case. Only a limited number of people could have enough control to let a murderer walk, and he was facing one of them right now.

No time to hesitate, I have to move forward. I have to trust this guy. He has never been one to betray a trust or skirt the law before as far as Danny knew. That had not been the case for one Detective Lieutenant.

Chapter 39

Danny was no longer ready to head to forestry school, at least not until he took care of some unfinished business. All the bad thoughts he had about Supervising District Attorney Marvin Cohen were mostly gone, and the old image was returning. *That little bastard would have made a great Marine*, he thought. *I hope to God he is on my side. If he isn't, then I am in real trouble. Now let's hope this cover up doesn't run too deep.*

Most of the people in the police department were intimidated by Detective Lieutenant Snyder and would roll over to his demands, that didn't extend to lying and covering up a murder. How many people however, would soon have a case of amnesia and not want to get involved? It's one thing to lie. Then there are people who suddenly can't remember things, details. This is a small town, and secrets are hard to keep. Someone in the know with information about Brad and Penny's life style or what he or Penny said would eventually get out. Swinging, cheating, jealousy, rage, divorce, alimony— maybe it was just making Brad look like a fool that caused him to go get the shotgun and blow Penny's brains out. If any of the swinging was true, then someone would be bragging. If someone knew what was going on and wasn't getting in on the action, then there would be the jealous talk. In a line from an old gangster movie, *three people could keep a secret so long as two of them were dead.* Someone knew, and someone would talk. Brad had that kind of a temper and when it came down to it; Penny could be a terror from what Danny had been told. He had never seen it; he had heard she could be a raging bitch. Who knows what was said that night or why. Only two people know for sure, one is dead and the other is lying through his teeth.

A lot was going to depend on how many people were willing to stand up and tell the truth. The story was so sordid that Penny's family just wanted everything to go away. Protecting Penny's memory made the family feel that putting all this behind them was better than getting justice for their daughter. What had they been told that could make them have the kind of thoughts to just be done with this? Where are all the people who were close to Penny besides her family who would want to see her murderer punished? Were there that many secrets in this small town to make people stop caring? Were some of the so-called friends so worried that their secrets would be revealed that they would write off the life of someone they knew and liked and, maybe even loved?

Danny wasn't a close friend—bus rides to school, seeing her at the high school, a few words every now and then in passing. There had never been a relationship or even the thought of a relationship. Penny had always been Brad's girl going back as far as Danny could remember. His days in the Marines left a six-year gap of the unknown. In that span of time, life had moved on in Maidstone, and Danny had not been part of it. He had grown up in the Marines, all over the world. Violence at times for Danny was common place. The town of Maidstone, to the returning Marine hadn't changed more than a few days in six years. People were older, but they hadn't aged the way a Marine does. Danny thought of the days where work lasted more than twenty-four hours. Weekends were something Marines remembered, just never had. Holidays when possible were a special meal and that was it. On the surface Maidstone hadn't changed. The people of Maidstone had grown up and still looked almost the same as they did in high school. Danny was from town, and now he was a police officer. He hadn't been part of that quiet inside change. While still a hometown boy, he hadn't been around to be part of that closed community bonding. He wasn't on the outside looking in. His time away and now a police officer; limited his view of the town. He would go to parties or see friends in a bar around the Berkshires and would always get a warm greeting. Then Danny noticed things would always get quiet when he came around. He was a Marine, he was the police, and he was not to be let into the secret society that had evolved in Maidstone while he was away. Maybe it was the parties where recreational drugs came out. Maybe it was the swinging or cheating or the business bonds good and bad that had been built up while he was away. Whatever it was, he was kept at a distance, not a long distance, just on the other side of the line. At first, he kind of resented being left out. Now he was glad he wasn't on the inside.

As Cohen directed, Danny did his duty and from time to time would bad mouth the District Attorney's Office. Even so he couldn't get a conversation going. He would bring up points of evidence of Brad's guilt that the District Attorney's Office had overlooked. He rarely got any more input than an agreement or a shrug from people who should have known the facts and made a more detailed comment. He was fishing, he wasn't catching. Then one day he was told to report to the Detective Lieutenant's office. His first thought was, *oh shit I'm toast*. Now he had to play the dummy and walked right up to the Lieutenant's door.

"You asked to see me, sir."

"Yes, come in and shut the door."

200

This is not good, thought Danny, *just stay cool, stay ice friggin cold*. He went in, sat down, and asked, "What can I do for you, Sir?"

"First off," began the Detective Lieutenant, "you have to stop bad mouthing the District Attorney's Office right now."

That was the one thing Danny never expected to hear from Detective Lieutenant Snyder.

"Yes, sir" was his response, "but they screwed the case up royally."

"Whatever they did or didn't do, it's over now. There's no going back. They did what they decided to do for whatever reason, and we have to live with it. If you keep telling people how screwed up they are then the rest of us will pay for it the next time we go to court or we need a search or arrest warrant. You follow me so far?"

"Yes sir," was Danny's response, of course he knew the real reason.

"Just let this whole thing be a bad memory and let people forget about it and stop talking about it."

The sooner that happened, the sooner the heat would be off Detective Lieutenant Snyder. Snyder's life could get back to normal with fewer people looking over his shoulder and asking questions. If Danny kept bringing the case up and bad mouthing the District Attorney's Office, eventually it would get back to Marvin Cohen. Cohen would have a sit down with Danny and his attitude. Things that weren't supposed to come out might get exposed and that was the last thing that Snyder wanted.

Too late, thought Danny. *That cat is out of the bag, and he doesn't know it*. Danny still had to wonder if Cohen has anything to do with this.

"Sir, I will keep my mouth shut. You know it still sucks."

"Yes, it does. I agree with you completely. Now it's over. Forget about it, move on. Got it?"

"Yes sir."

"Thanks, you're dismissed."

To Danny's great relief, he was on his way out the door sooner than he had hoped congratulating himself on what he hoped would be his first and last grand performance.

Chapter 40

Danny got to class early so he could have some time with District Attorney Cohen. He was hoping for an update and maybe some good news. What he got was all bad.

"Danny, come in and close the door. We need to make this quick so you can get out and come back after some of the other students arrive. People are starting to talk, and they think you're trying to re-open the case and to a lesser extent, that I am involved. Have you been bringing the subject up at the station?"

"Yes kind of, not really," was the qualified answer. "I've been asking people about somethings that happened that night that they were directly involved in to see what they remembered or what they are going to say on the record. Like I asked the Dispatcher about Brad saying that he just killed his wife, and the Dispatcher coached his answer by saying it was a crazy night and he wasn't sure of what he'd heard. I don't know if someone had a chat with him or if he really doesn't remember or doesn't want to get involved. It wasn't like I was interrogating anyone. Other people are talking about the case too, so I'm not the only one who has shown an interest. I did get called into Lieutenant Snyder's office and was told to stop bad-mouthing you and the District Attorney's Office and to forget the whole thing."

"Well, there have been calls to my office—not to me personally, to other people checking on things. They were asking if anyone has requested the court file or if there was a transcript of the sentencing. One of the people in the office has some connection with the department and took the request, she didn't tell me. I found out because the person who took the call made a note of the request and I happened to see it. For the time being, cool it with the fishing expedition. Try not to draw attention to yourself. Now scram and don't come in until you see several students in here and no meeting after class. I will be in touch and don't call the office. Here is my cell number. If you need to talk, call that number and do not use any of the department phones including the department's cell phone."

"This is sounding a bit too James Bond. This is Maidstone not New York City."

"There might be something more here than we know," said Attorney Cohen. "The FBI wants to see me, and this is the only thing I have going right now. I don't know the connection between Brad and a domestic murder and why the FBI would want to talk me. They want to see me in person and not talk over the phone or in my office. I don't know if there is a connection, and I can't see one, just be careful. Now go."

Danny was wondering what the FBI knew and why a federal agency would get involved in a purely local crime? He couldn't think of any federal statute that had been violated. Was Cohen trying to scare him? Danny wanted to trust him; things were so crazy at this point. He wasn't sure who he could trust.

Danny left the classroom and didn't see anyone in the hall. He reached around to the small of his back and out of habit, adjusted his Beretta 380 auto that was tucked in his waistband. It was clipped in securely, and he made sure that the sweatshirt was covering it. He wasn't supposed to be carrying a firearm in class. The fact that he was a police officer didn't matter. Lately he was doing a lot of things he shouldn't be doing. Out of habit he had purchased the Beretta when he got on the force. For six years as a Marine he had carried a Beretta 92-F, and old habits die hard. It was smaller than the 92-F, still it felt right in his hand. Well, he trusted the Beretta. He felt good about it. Now he was trusting Marvin Cohen. He hoped he was right on both counts.

Danny got a coffee and moved back towards the classroom and stayed at the far end of the hall. He had the feeling he was being watched, he just couldn't identify by who. Maybe I am just being paranoid, then again, if someone really is after you then you're not paranoid, you're a realist. After six years of knowing someone was trying to kill you, it was easy to think that the threat was still there.

A few people walked by and into the classroom. They exchanged the usual greetings, nothing out of the ordinary. After several people had entered, Danny went in to the classroom and took a seat to the rear and off to one side. He gave Supervising District Attorney Cohen a dirty look and shook his head in a negative manner just in case someone was watching. He wanted people to think he still had a hard-on for the little bastard that let Brad walk.

At the end of class he grabbed his books and was the first one out the door. If anyone was watching, they would know that he hadn't stuck around to chat it up with the professor.

Danny and Attorney Cohen didn't know that it was already too late. The wheels were in motion. The train had left the station, and it was on a collision course with the two of them. Over the next few days, Danny didn't have a reason to call Supervising District Attorney Cohen, so he never knew about a secret meeting that had taken place with the FBI. Soon Danny would be included, for now, everything was cool. There was no reason to put him on guard or tip the hand about information that would put Brad behind bars for ten years or more and possibly a dozen other people as well. If Danny started looking over his shoulder more than most cops, it could ruin a great plan.

The FBI loved big orchestrated take-downs with dozens of agents. The press release was done before they headed out for the raid. Certain newspaper and media contacts would have an inside track and might even be on scene when the bust went down. The FBI loved positive press and always looked to make sure their image was portrayed in the most favorable light. Any soldier or Marine knows that any great plan does not survive first contact. The assholes always have a vote in spite of the best laid plans. Anything can turn to shit in a heartbeat. Danny had a great sixth sense in reading trouble. He was also lucky. He was going to need both if he wanted to make it to the weekend.

Chapter 41

On the night of February 9, 2010, the snow was falling. The town had returned to its quiet Berkshire self. The traffic had slowed to a crawl, what there was of it. Most of the town was asleep. There hadn't been one call for any of the units since they had started their shift. Finally Danny was dispatched to check out a running car at the Shell Station. *At least I now have something to make it look like I am earning my pay*, thought Danny.

"Unit one," said Danny into the microphone. "I will be out of the car at the Shell Station; so far I have not located the vehicle."

"Roger," was the clipped response.

And the FBI's plan turned to shit in that instant. Here was the hi-tech, spare-no-expense FBI that never considered that a small New England town might have poor cell phone reception.

The Town of Maidstone for whatever reason had horrible cell phone service. Standing at one spot then moving one hundred yards away could mean a dropped call. Having your cell phone on the dashboard, you might get service. If the phone was on the seat and in the computer case, forget it. None of the FBI take-down teams were in place. They were all asleep when the monitoring team intercepted the call to Detective Lieutenant Snyder that the hit was going down right now. Even Snyder was surprised. He had to get dressed fast so that he could get out and take control of the scene to make sure things went as planned. The Detective Lieutenant wasn't prepared for this. He had to get moving if he cared to stay out of jail.

Unfortunately for Danny, the warning call from the FBI never made it through. Danny Gilcrest had just driven into a trap and now was completely on his own.

After the ambush, the series of medical tests kept Danny at the hospital for hours. He arrived back at the scene shortly after the State Police Major Case Squad and saw the mess. He looked across the landscape that had once been a few inches of dry pristine snow that was now nothing but foot prints and tire tracks. Near the train station he saw that the news crews were setting up their satellite trucks in the parking lot where the getaway car had been parked. He looked around for Detective Lieutenant Snyder. He was nowhere to be found. Several anonymous calls had been made to the TV and radio stations about the attempted murder of a Maidstone police officer. Every news crew poured into the tiny New England town from as far away as Boston and New York City.

Danny asked where Officer Gary Carlson was and was told he was up on Route 9 at Main Street directing traffic.

"Who interviewed him," Danny asked.

No one knew. He made his way the short distance to Main Street, to find Gary.

"What the hell are you doin?" Danny asked.

"Flappin my arms for the last six hours, and I need to take a leak. How are you doing?"

"Has anyone interviewed you?"

"No," was the quick reply.

"Well, no one came to the hospital to see me to find out what happened. How long have the State Police been here?"

"They just pulled in."

This could not be happening, thought Danny. *Now they want me dead. Could Brad and Snyder really put out a contract on me?*

"Hey," called out a State Police Lieutenant, "are you Gilcrest?"

"Yes," was the sunken reply.

"The District Attorney is very concerned about you. From now on you're staying with us, and we need to talk," said the Lieutenant.

"No shit," said Danny, "no shit."

A State Trooper wearing a raid jacket was heading to the Major Crime van with several bags that looked like evidence.

"Hey," Danny called out. "What've you got?"

"Some evidence seized by your department."

"Like what," asked Danny?

"There's a coffee cup, a cigarette butt, some paper, and a bag with a soda can in it."

"Can I see the coffee cup and the cigarette?" asked Danny. "I was the one who got shot at?"

"Sure, just don't touch—we need to dust for prints."

Danny looked into the two bags, and his heart sank. The coffee cup was cardboard not Styrofoam. The cigarette butt had a white filter not a brown one. These were not the items he and Gary had seen when they had followed the tracks to the shooter's position.

The State Police Detective Lieutenant walked Danny over to a large, newer Ford Crown Vic with deeply tinted windows. The Trooper kept looking around and gave the impression that he was a Secret Service Agent on a protection detail. Danny wondered who this guy was looking for. He doubted that whoever shot at him last night was still around. Even if they were, there were just too many troopers and police officers to try something. Seeing that no one was looking in their direction, the Trooper opened the back door just enough so that Danny could slip in. Danny actually had a hard time getting in the door because it was only opened about half way. As he slipped into the seat, Danny came face to face with Attorney Cohen. Their eyes locked, and Cohen was the first to speak.

"Danny, first off, let me say I am sorry. The up side is, of course, you didn't get hurt and everyone is okay."

Danny was confused. "Why are you telling me you're sorry?"

"Danny, this is going to take some time to explain. I am going to give you every single detail."

Danny looked at Cohen for the longest time trying to read his face and digest what he had just said.

"Did you know someone was going to try and kill me and didn't tell me?"

"The short, dirty answer is yes. It wasn't our idea to let this go so far to the point where someone shot at you. Things got out of hand for the dumbest of reasons. Like I said, it's going to take some explaining. I am still very sorry, I am glad that everything turned out okay and everyone is fine."

"Everyone is fine? Who's everyone?" Danny wanted to know. Before he got a response, the two men in the front seat decided it was time to make their introductions.

"We are with the FBI Field Office in Boston, and we are very pleased to make your acquaintance."

Oh, shit, thought Danny, the FBI. No wonder I almost got killed. Then again what would the FBI be doing here so soon, and who is everyone that's okay? What could Penny's murder have to do with the FBI?

"Danny," began Attorney Cohen, " when you and I started looking into the bag job that got Brad seven years' probation, we had no idea the hornet's nest we kicked over."

Here was a hit on a police officer and the FBI was involved—they knew it was going to go down, and Danny hadn't been warned. Where did Brad get the connections for a hit? The questions were coming faster than the answers. Besides, Brad had gotten seven years' probation and double jeopardy would apply, so he was golden.

"Why kill me for asking questions?"

Attorney Cohen continued, "Brad was just a side show to the main event. His arrest and probation got your attention and by extension, mine. That began bringing scrutiny on Detective Lieutenant Snyder. That in turn threatened some major players unassociated with Brad, but with close ties to

211

the Detective Lieutenant. Snyder thought that picking up a few bucks for bagging Brad's case was worth it because who would question what went down. No one would find out that he threw the case. That is until you started poking around and then you came after me. These things, this questioning of the case, got a third party very nervous that had nothing to do with Penny and Brad. It had everything to do with Snyder and some people with a lot of vowels in their last names."

"I guess this is where I come in," said the FBI Agent in the passenger's seat. "I am Special Agent Shawn Jones in charge of the Boston Field Office for Organized Crime."

Danny was at a loss for just about everything at this point. Why if Brad's killing Penny had nothing to do with the mob and Detective Lieutenant Snyder got paid off to bag the case was there a hit put out on him? Danny kept looking from one agent to the other and then back at Attorney Cohen.

"OK, what the hell is going on?"

Agent Jones began. "The short version is that you and Attorney Cohen figured out that Snyder had bagged the case, and it was about to blow up on him. He would first off lose his job, and in all likelihood do some serious time."

"So, he ordered a hit?" asked Danny.

"No, the mob did," replied Agent Jones.

"The mob had nothing to do with Penny and Brad, so how did they get involved?" asked Danny.

"We found that your Detective Lieutenant Snyder has been leading a double life. With the two of you about ready to expose him, his friends in the mob became extremely concerned. You see, your Lieutenant likes to gamble, and he's not very good at it and loses a lot."

Danny remembered seeing the Lieutenant at one of the gas stations buying all kinds of lottery tickets. *How could that bring in the mob?* "Lottery tickets got him jammed up?" asked Danny.

"If he had stayed with the lottery," said Jones, "he might have been okay. But no, he liked to bet on everything: basketball, football, horse racing anything that you could put money down on, his big down fall was poker. Cards were where he took the big hit. You see he would get into these backroom games down in New York City or up in the Catskills, and for a while he was always winning. His winning wasn't because he had great luck or skill, but because the games were all rigged. The city boys needed some inside law enforcement information away from the NYPD and saw him as a good mark. With all his years up in the Berkshires, he had great contacts for gathering information that the mob wanted. He loved hanging with the wise guys. There was the money, cars, and babes; and at the time he was winning. He got used to the extra money. This changed his lifestyle and he now he thought of himself as a high-roller as the mob had planned. Then there was the occasional favor they would ask of him. Nothing really illegal, just something an officer shouldn't have done. Money exchanged hands, and at that point he was inside their grasp. Then, he started losing at cards. They were all his 'friends' so, no big deal. They would let his losses ride. They gave him a pass right up until he could never get out of debt. Then they dropped the hammer on him. They had Snyder on audio and video gambling and losing. They had him the same way taking money for favors and signing markers for debts. They recorded the Detective Lieutenant relaying restricted law enforcement information that he shouldn't have so they made him the proverbial offer that he couldn't refuse. Work for them and the markers will be forgotten and, you can keep on gambling. Of course, they were ready to make sure he was justly compensated for his efforts. Truth be told, we do the same thing when we go after the mob or in another unit that is after people committing espionage for a foreign power. It's the same way we flip informants."

Danny was listening; he just couldn't believe that a Detective Lieutenant from Maidstone, Massachusetts, could be of any value to organized crime. This was the FBI and the way they were talking there was more to come.

Special Agent Jones continued. "Some of the requests were simple, like running a plate or checking on someone off the record. At some point, they had him open his own investigation agency to cover his inquires. He had the company in someone else's name, but it was Detective Lieutenant Snyder all the way. One of the big things he did was arrange safe houses for meetings and getaways for the boys. They liked being able to make a call and have a real safe house waiting for them. Snyder through his security company had access to dozens of homes, estates, inns, and out buildings to offer them. People who had second homes or investment properties up here liked the idea that a police lieutenant from the area was watching their houses. He worked with the real estate management people to have access to these homes. Most of these properties are only used by their owners a few weeks of every year, if at all. The rest of the time they are vacant. The ones he was interested in were rented out. Snyder would get a call from the city that they needed a place for a certain date, and he would make the arrangements. No one, including us, knew which place it would be until the boys hit town. Then they would call Snyder and find out where to go. He also had arrangements with caterers and other venders. With the money the boys had; it was no problem getting the place stocked on short notice. Our problem was that we couldn't get someone in with the caterers because we never knew which one Snyder would pick. We asked the US Attorney for permission to bug several places, but we couldn't tell them which one specifically until it was too late to get someone in to place the bugs. The US Attorney wouldn't let us plant bugs in a few dozen locations hoping that one of them would be the next meeting place. Long-range wiretaps that we did get didn't work because they would use a series of burn phones or encrypted emails. You even pulled security at some of these meetings and didn't know it. Remember all those special details where some big wig was coming up and didn't want to be disturbed?"

"Now keep in mind that this was a cash-only business. All the deliveries were paid for in cash and well above the going rate. The purveyors were more than happy to jump through a few hoops for this kind of deal. The real estate property managers were the worst. If they knew the owners were out of town and not coming up, they would pocket the rental fee for themselves. These little side deals were very profitable and a great way to keep people from talking. No one wanted to screw up a sweet, off-the-books cash deal like this."

Jones was making a good case. Still Danny was finding it hard to accept that all this was going on in Maidstone. He thought back on some of those cake assignments. All he had to do was hang around the main driveway and keep people away. It was boring; it was also time and a half. Sometimes there was a bonus of a free meal. Half the time he didn't know who he was protecting. People would arrive in a limo or a huge SUV, and the driver would check in. That would be the last he saw of anyone. There were rumors that movie stars and real estate giants had been up to the Berkshires as well as bankers, corporate CEOs, you name it. Some were friendly and talked with the officers, and others

215

were never seen. Danny recalled a few details when the personal security people were a little rough around the edges. On top of that, they didn't like cops.

"I do recall some tough types," said Danny. "I thought they were like security for rappers or something. I never made the connection."

"Oh, these were high-profile people to be sure, and some might have had business with the people you mentioned. Most were in the waste management business or the trade unions or specialized wagering, real specialized wagering. Our problem was that we didn't know who knew or didn't know what was going on. While Snyder is the main player up here, there probably is more than one contact. In all likelihood, there are others associated with the police."

"If Snyder was going down, then why didn't they whack him instead of me? If he was gone the connection would be gone and end of story," said Danny.

"Excellent point," said Jones. "While Snyder couldn't gamble for shit, he did hedge his bets with the mob. He bugged the mob better than we could. He recorded every meeting. The first time the boys came up, he watched them do a sweep for bugs. In that time, he found their flaw. The mob boys were so busy looking for hi-tech FBI bugs they never checked for the low-tech stuff. He used old fashioned tape recorders with real tape that were remotely activated after they had made a sweep for the bugs. The low-tech stuff didn't give off an electronic signature that could be detected by the equipment the mobs counter-surveillance people used. After the meetings broke up, he would go in and retrieve the recordings and make a bunch of copies. He would then drop off packages at UPS stores with a stipulation that if the bill wasn't paid for storage every thirty days, they were to ship them to the addresses on the packages. It was all prepaid and a great insurance policy. He never put anything on the address that would make a clerk suspicious. He might use my name and the physical address of the FBI Field Office with no mention of the FBI. If things went south for him in thirty days, I would have a package. We never knew about the tapes until we picked him up, and he wanted a deal. He hinted about real hard evidence against the city boys in exchange for some leniency. It was *let's make a deal time."*

Danny was starting to question everything that was going on. This wasn't the Maidstone where he grew up in, and all this couldn't possibly be happening in the Berkshires. Danny was trying to form a question when State Police Detective Lieutenant Ronnie Cavanaugh got in to the back seat with him. He knew Lieutenant Cavanaugh from several golf tournaments. Danny never played he just always helped out as part of the support. Cavanaugh was not known as a great golfer, and most people were very nervous when he had a club in his hands. As he slipped into the seat, he announced, "She's okay and on her way out of town."

"Who is she?" Danny asked.

Cavanaugh looked at him and said, "Trooper Anyzeski."

Danny was stunned and felt like he had just hit his head all over again. "What do mean Geri is all right and on her way out of town. What happened to her?"

Cavanaugh looked disapprovingly at the two FBI agents.

"We hadn't gotten that far," said Special Agent Jones.

Danny kept looking from the agents to the attorney to Cavanaugh, and no one was speaking.

"What the hell is going on?" he demanded.

Special Agent Jones took a deep breath and spoke slowly trying to bring the tension down. "You were not the only one who was to be hit."

All Danny could think of was *shit*.

"So, what happened to Geri?"

"Geri's name came up, and there was talk about breaking into her apartment to make it look like a home invasion. When it looked like they had taken you out, the shooter started making phones calls. His first call was to Lieutenant Snyder to get down to the scene and take charge. You see the results of that in front of you. A second call was made to take out Geri. A third call was to a guy waiting outside Attorney Cohen's house. Attorney Cohen was supposed to trip over a shoe lace and fall down his back stairs, hit his head, and die. We intercepted the call to Lieutenant Snyder and learned what was supposed to be happening next. Unfortunately, we didn't have anyone in place. The hit was not supposed to go down until Friday."

"A call was made to Geri to warn her to get out of there. At first, she didn't believe it. When she saw the SUV with the tinted windows pull into the parking lot she dropped the phone. The next thing we heard was the sound of the door getting kicked in followed by a single gunshot. That was followed by two more shots in quick succession. The first guy through the door took the hit right in the snot locker. The second guy never got his gun up and took two hits dead nuts in the K-5. They never got off a round.

"Your apartment was going to be broken into, in such a way that the break-in wouldn't be detected and your computer and files were going to disappear. Your buddy, Bear, didn't see it that way and took a chunk out of the guy's leg and hand. For a Labrador, he was mighty feisty."

"Where are Geri and Bear now?" Danny wanted to know.

"He is on his way out of town with Geri," said Cavanaugh. "She is just fine and so is Bear."

More questions were racing into his mind, and he shot them out faster than they could listen.

Chapter 42

"Slow down, please," said Special Agent Jones. "We are going to tell you everything. There's a lot to it and will take time. Hang in there and listen. We got word from a wiretap down in the city that a Supervising District Attorney, a cop and a trooper were going to get whacked. We figured out it was Attorney Cohen and had him come in. Based on what he was doing at the time and the fact that a cop and a female state trooper were also in the mix, we came up with you. This was two weeks ago."

"You knew we were going to be killed in a mob hit two weeks ago and didn't think I should know about it?"

Danny was about to go over the seat and start beating the crap out of two FBI agents. He thought of the boom the shotgun had made, and the only reason he was still alive was that he fell on his ass getting out of the cruiser.

Cavanaugh felt him making his move to go over the seat and with a strong arm, restrained him and spoke softly and slowly into his ear.

"Hang on there is more, a lot more; and after they finish, we can both kick the shit out of them if you like."

Danny was far from cool about waiting. If there was more, he wanted to hear it.

Jones could understand that he just might deserve getting pounded. He hoped that the next few minutes would change the big guy's mind.

"When we found out about the scheduled hits and the break in, we dispatched agents up here and contacted the State Police."

Danny's head swung around and glared at Cavanaugh. "You mother fucker, you knew and didn't tell Geri?"

"Please keep listening," said Cavanaugh.

Jones continued. "Once we knew the players, we put GPS tracking devices on your cars and put real-time video surveillance on your homes. We were watching, 24/7."

"You still didn't stop them from almost gunning me down!" shouted Danny.

"That's because the hit was supposed to go down on Friday not three days before on Tuesday."

"So, there was a scheduling conflict?" demanded Danny.

"In a manner of speaking, yes, the city boys ordered the hit for Friday. They in turn told Snyder it would be Friday. He was part of the plan to make sure the crime scene was compromised. What we didn't know was that the guy putting the hit team together ran into some problems. One guy was scheduled for a colonoscopy on Friday and another guy on the hit team had to be at his daughter's concert at Finnery and Grant Hall in Wallingford, Connecticut, on Saturday. So, without telling the city boys the change in plans, they made their move early, figuring that the day didn't matter. They would call Snyder and give him enough time to get to the scene, take over, and keep the State Police away."

Danny was hearing and not believing that a recital and a colonoscopy almost got him killed and that the FBI had this

221

big plan to take down a hit team and had the wrong fucking day.

"And Geri, Bear and Attorney Cohen?" asked Danny.

"We were monitoring everything in real time. Once we intercepted the call to Snyder and they took the shot at you, we began to move. Troopers got to your place seconds after the guy made his way into the barn, just not before Bear sunk his teeth into him. Attorney Cohen was supposed to be taken down when he responded to your untimely death or when he headed to work. Agents grabbed the guy with the baseball bat before he could do any harm. He tried to claim he was just out for a walk and carried the bat for protection. The one thing that broke our way was the timing. Geri, Cohen and the break-in at your place were set to go down after they were sure that you had been taken out. We were almost too late at the barn, of course Bear handled things for us. So, yes, it's a mess; and, yes, we really screwed up; and, yes, we are sorry. The up side is that Snyder is talking up a storm trying to cut a deal. We have any number of wise guys on tape talking about everything from other made men's wives to contract hits on Snyder's seized tapes."

"So where are Geri and Bear off to?" asked Danny.

"Remember that quiet little Inn up in Franconia Notch, Lovett's?" said Special Agent Jones.

Danny did remember it fondly along with memories of Geri. "Yes, I do."

"She's on her way up there for a stay. At some point she'll be assigned to Fort Devens and work with the FBI/State Police Joint Organized Crime Task Force. The inn is out of the way. The owners are former government employees and know how to be discreet. Geri will have her own cottage with Bear and can get out and not be seen by a whole lot of people. It's a great place not to be noticed. A couple of agents will be with her 24/7, and the State Police will be doing some debriefing along with us. We still have to sort out who isn't playing for our team up here in the Berkshires. So, while that is going on, you and Attorney Cohen are going to have things to do in other parts of the country. You are going to grow a beard, and we are going to change Geri's appearance somehow. As far as you're concerned, you have just been accepted into the FBI National Academy for a two-and-a-half-month training course down in Quantico, Virginia. Most of your time will be spent being debriefed; the school is a good cover. Plus, it's in the middle of a Marine Base with a few hundred cops and agents and should be safe."

Danny was taking it all in, still processing all the information that had just been dumped on him. His thoughts of beating the crap out of two FBI Agents had somewhat faded, though it wasn't completely gone. He wanted to see Geri to prove to himself that she was all right. He needed his dog, and Geri. That seemed to be out of the question.

"With the cat out of the bag with Snyder, the chances that the city boys will come after you again are remote. Their beef wasn't with you; it was with Snyder getting exposed and talking. Now that he's been compromised, keeping you and Geri quiet is an empty cause for them. Of course they don't know he's talking just yet. We are reasonably sure you're safe. Just in case, we want all three of you out of town for a while."

"Why did they want to take out Geri?" asked Danny. "She had no part in it."

"Somehow, they figured she knew what was going on, at least that was part of the conversation that we intercepted. Maybe you talked about it to her. Whatever the reason, the boys or Snyder made the connection and decided she had to go, too.

"So, what happens to Brad," Danny wanted to know. "Is he off the hook with double jeopardy seeing that he's already been convicted?"

"Not at all," said Attorney Cohen, "not by a long shot. We don't have him connected to the hit. He isn't protected under double jeopardy because he lied under oath when he told what had happened. So, he can be tried all over again, this time with the real evidence. He's also looking at lying on the stand and conspiracy, so we will have a lot of leverage to get him to roll over. He's going to do more than seven years. We have to see what his story is and if he's willing to talk. Then we will have to evaluate if he is being truthful this time. Right now we are looking at murder, and there will be no deals. He either takes what we offer, or we go to trial for the max."

Chapter 43

Danny had heard about the FBI National Academy. For the most part, it was for senior police officers who would be the leaders of their departments in the higher ranks. Maidstone might have sent someone who was being groomed for chief, not a junior patrolman. The nice thing was that anyone from Maidstone who heard about Danny getting into the school decided that after almost being killed, he deserved a break, and no one would be asking any questions.

Detective Lieutenant Snyder's departure was also easily explained away as he was recuperating from a heart attack. He probably had some kind of heart event when the FBI and State Police picked him up, that did not require hospitalization. It was ironic that Snyder and Geri would both end up at Fort Devens, of course in separate areas of the facility. Snyder would never see the outside for several months if ever, and their paths would never cross. That was a plus for Snyder because the first thing that Geri said was that she still had the 38-snub nose with three rounds, and she knew just where to put them. Snyder was talking, and the FBI wanted to keep the city boys in the dark as long as possible before they rounded them up. They had teams listening to hours of audio tapes. Agents were sifting through the BS to get the information they could act on. There were hours of tape, and it takes hours to listen to all the conversations. That left a lot of editing to cut the important stuff from the BS and make a case. Listening to the tapes just one time was not going to be enough; this wasn't going to be over anytime soon.

District Attorney Cohen found himself lecturing at police academies in various parts of the country on ethics and police procedure. There wasn't one student not paying attention. The lectures were dynamic, even more so than before. He spoke of the events in Maidstone in a way that they could not be connected to him or what was known in the recent past. With Snyder locked up, Cohen would soon be back in Berkshire County raising hell, only after Snyder's associates in western Massachusetts were identified and picked up.

The FBI for their part had everyone on ice. The city boys were in a panic. One of the four guys on the hit team was missing, and his whereabouts unknown to the city boys. Two had been reported killed in a home invasion. Their major mole in Berkshire County was in the hospital, and they couldn't contact him, or so they had been told. With the city boys trying to piece things together, the result was there were people making phone calls and talking in inappropriate places. These conversations led to even more information and details about the mob's activities. For the FBI, it was all on the plus side by accident. When this was all over, and the mutts were rounded up, there would be no mention of their major screw ups. The press release would laud the FBI for its innovation and exemplary investigative skills. They already had one great press release prepared. A simple rewrite would not be able to correct the mistakes, so they had to start fresh. You can only do so much with cut and paste.

Danny was very impressed with the National Academy and he had been by it a few times in the past, and it looked like a new university not a government building. It was a full-

226

size training campus with everything including a beer hall. The inside was even better. The classrooms and the visual aids were all top shelf. The instructors were all FBI agents or senior FBI technicians with law degrees or Doctorates in their respective fields. This was the best of the best that the FBI had to offer. Danny still did not have a lot of trust in the FBI after almost getting him killed. Still he could not ignore how good the National Academy was. He spent time with the organized crime unit; though he had little to offer in the way of information. The Behavioral Science guys were something else. They picked Danny's brain about the events, and also about his time in the Marines. Every aspect of his life was exposed. They found it interesting that with no intentions of ever being a police officer, he had become one. Now that Danny was posted at the National Academy and not Bob Marshalls School of Forestry a frequent question was, "So what are you going to do now?"

Danny's answer, "No idea."

One of the debriefing agents asked Danny if he had ever been to The Major's Place just outside of Quantico?

"Yes," Danny replied, "it was a mistake."

"How so?" asked the agent.

"I thought it was a bar and a restaurant, and it is sort of. If there is an event going on and you're invited, you get to stand at the bar and have a drink. If there isn't an event, then the bar isn't used. You are there for dinner and not to have a few pops. I didn't know it when I went in, and walked up to the bar and asked for a scotch. I got the scotch and was escorted to a table and informed that the bar wasn't open. Then the Major explained that this was a for real Marine establishment with a twist. No one was coming in here to drink Bud and pound down shots of Jägermeister. There would be no loud conversations or four-letter words. This was where ladies and gentlemen of the Marine Corps family would come for a prime rib dinner, a glass of single malt scotch, and a bottle of a fine wine. This was not a bucket of blood where young Marines proved how tough they were. This was an honored place run by a long-time Marine for the enjoyment of Marines and their families. It was the best, all top shelf. If anyone wanted to change the rules, the Major sent them packing. It was the Major's establishment, and he made the rules."

"So, what happened?" asked the agent.

"I raised my glass to the Major and thanked him for setting me straight. I promised him that I would finish my scotch and be on my way. I thanked him for the hospitality and the education. I promised him that the next time I was back I would be in the company of a lovely young lady to enjoy a fine night out enjoying a prime rib. We shook hands, and we parted. That was the last time I was there. I never did get a prime rib."

"If that's the case," said the Agent, "then we need to get you back there. I will take you out to dinner, and we won't remind the Major of the young lady part."

"I doubt that the Major would remember me. A prime rib does sound good. I would also like a second look at the place. There is so much history there that I want to see. My last visit was somewhat abbreviated. I'd like to get a look at everything in there".

"Great, I will make reservations for seven and pick you up at the main lobby where you can sign out at six."

"Deal."

They made their way to The Majors Place, with very little conversation. The countryside was very bleak and grey, no leaves on the trees, and no snow on the ground. The darkness only added to the gloom.

The agent pulled up to the front of The Major's Place and told Danny to go ahead as he had several private phone calls to make.

"Just give them my name; they have the reservation." Walking in Danny took in all the Marine Corps memorabilia and artifacts, some going back over 150 years. It was a great place and gave both a feeling of history and comfort. There is a heritage not all the services shared across the board in the Marines, Private to Commandant. Yes, this was the real Marine Corps. It felt more like walking into someone's den than a restaurant. Danny felt honored just to be allowed in the place. A Private graduating from Parris Island would be called a Marine on that final day of training. The Commandant of the Marine Corps on that very same day would also be called a Marine. At that moment and for eternity, they would forever share that bond that they were Marines. Danny felt that bond when he walked through that door.

The Major came over and extended his hand and said, "Welcome back, Danny, it is good to see you again."

Danny took the extended hand and could not believe that the Major had any clue who he was. It was still nice to think that he might have.

"Someone will be joining you this time, I trust."

"Yes, there are two of us. My dinner partner had to make some phone calls and will be in shortly."

"Excellent, this way please," and Danny was directed to a table in the back.

Danny was headed for the far side of the table so that he would be facing the door. The Major directed him to the chair on the opposite side. He hesitated for a moment; the look on the Major's face told him that your seat was where he directed you. After the first brief encounter years ago, Danny knew that doing what the Major requested was a good thing and went a long way to a gentlemanly relationship.

"A waitress will be with you shortly," said the Major and abruptly turned and disappeared into the back room.

Danny was a bit uncomfortable sitting facing a wall with his back to the door. Every fiber in his body was directing him to get up and change seats. He hesitated just long enough looking at the pictures on the wall of dozens of Marines from before he was born smiling back at him. A glass appeared in front of him.

"I didn't order anything," Danny said.

The waitress smiled sweetly and said. "This one was on the Major. He was sure you'd like it. If not, I can always take it back. He was sure you were a scotch drinker."

I am not about to piss off the Major, thought Danny; and he raised the glass in salute. Noticing that the glass was really ice cold and that it wasn't a glass after all but a small, shiny stainless-steel tumbler containing a very smooth scotch and no ice, he took a sip. *This is way out of my price range, I better sip it slowly and make it last.* As he went for his second sip, his left leg got bumped and something cold and wet was moving under his left hand.

"What the hell!" Danny pulled back and looked down to see a smiling, fat faced, yellow Labrador retriever looking up at him.

Danny almost dropped the scotch. "Bear, buddy, holy shit." He spun out of his chair and onto his knees to hug his dog. As he came out of the chair he noticed that the young lady he assumed was a dog handler who had brought Bear in was standing behind him. At first glance he saw that the handler had kind of an athletic build with short auburn hair done in a very stylishly with glasses to match. All of his focus was on Bear and the fact that he was all right and still smiling.

As he rubbed Bear's ears and face, he didn't notice that most of the people in the restaurant were concentrating on him. He was lost in his own little world that at that very moment was only about a three-foot circle. It was him and Bear and no one else existed until he heard a voice that broke through that tiny circle.

From above Danny heard, "Way to go, big fella, you sure know how to make a lady feel wanted."

Danny's head snapped back and looked past the cute dog handler trying to find Geri, there was no one there.

"Up here Jarhead," the dog handler implored.

By now there was some giggling going on in the restaurant and a few gasps.

Danny looked up, mouth agape, and into those soft blues eyes. He was totally confused by the glasses, the hair color, and the new sporty style. The voice was right. Where was the long blonde ponytail that he was so fond of watching bounce from side to side as Geri ran in front of him a lifetime ago? As he was getting to his feet, he recalled the agent saying that they were going to change Geri's appearance. Danny had guessed that it would be something simple, maybe the hair pulled back into a tight bun. The new look was a surprise, stunning, still a surprise.

He finally made it to his feet and hesitated for just a second. He wanted to just wrap his arms around her. After almost getting her killed, he wasn't sure how that would go.

Geri was getting just a tad impatient.

"If I don't get a hug in the next nanosecond, you are going to get kicked so hard you will never have kids."

That wasn't the opening Danny was looking for. It did remove all doubt what the next move should be, better be. Danny nearly crushed her with his embrace and was worried that he was hugging too hard—that is until she melted into him as close as she could and still be able to breath. Geri buried her head into his chest and wrapped her arms around him as tight as she could. Neither could see the tears forming in their eyes.

Without hesitation or any regret, Danny held her close and whispered in her ear, "I love you."

Quickly, Geri pulled back from his embrace just enough so that she could see his face. She needed to see the look in his eyes just to make sure that she had really heard what he said. Danny was ready to shit a brick when she pulled back thinking that he had once again screwed up. He had nothing to worry about.

Geri looked up at him knowing that he really meant it and said, "I wasn't ready for that. I really do like the sound of it."

Danny's little circle of the world had expanded just ever so slightly. It now included Geri along with Bear. It didn't go much beyond five feet from where they were standing. For all they knew, they were standing on the top of Mount Washington all alone with no one around for miles. Of course, they were in a tiny restaurant with fifty or so people looking on, taking in every move and word spoken. They had everyone's full attention as they stood there holding tight to each other with a fat face Labrador looking on.

Everyone at the Major's place figured that Danny was a Marine back from somewhere overseas. Now not many Marines have beards. The ones that do are usually doing something in a foreign land that no one knows about and no one is going to be asking any questions. That goes double for those that dine at The Major's Place. They knew better. Wherever it was that this Marine was coming back from, it was dangerous they could tell. The fact that it was Maidstone, Massachusetts, would've surprised them. Then again, they would never find that out. What was apparent was that this Marine, wherever he had been, was extremely missed by this beautiful young lady. Some of the people present remembered their own returns and embraces and saw their reflection in this couple. No one wanted to disturb the two. Danny and Geri were oblivious to their surroundings—that was until somewhere in the back, a lone person began to slowly clap. In short order, a second person joined in, followed by a third, and then everyone was on their feet. Danny and Geri came out of their trance. A bit embarrassed and wiping away the tears that had formed at the corner of their eyes, they gave a slight wave, and nodded their thanks to the crowd. The Major came over and pulled out Geri's chair for her. Without letting go of her left hand with his right, the two sat down. Instinctively their free hands went under the table. Bear finally got in on some of the attention.

"You really know how to show a girl a good time," said Geri.

"I really do love you," said Danny. "I meant it, all three words."

Danny thought she was going to break his fingers she held his hand so tight.

"I love you too," said Geri, at which point Bear was cuddling up to her just a bit more than Danny. That's OK— Danny liked her better than he like himself, so he couldn't blame Bear.

The prime rib was served; and during the entire meal, almost not a word was spoken. At the end, Danny asked for the check. The Major informed him that several of the other patrons had fought over the bill so that had been taken care of. As Danny began to rise to leave, the Major stopped him.

"You have cheesecake coming."

As he returned to his seat, Geri made a slight grimace and began to rub her back with her free hand which annoyed the heck out of Bear. "I think I need a back rub," Geri announced.

Danny looked across the table at Geri who was now giving just the slightest hint of a smile. Danny hesitated for a second then glanced up at the Major who was standing there awaiting a response.

"Could we get it to go?" said Danny. "We're in a bit of a hurry right now."

"Of course," said the Major, "of course," and he disappeared into the back room.

In a minute, they were out the door. Geri snuggled under Danny's arm and Bear trotting along right behind.

ALSO BY MARC YOUNGQUIST

THE 143rd IN IRAQ

The 143rd IN IRAQ is a military memoir detailing the combat deployment of a Connecticut Army National Guard Military Police Company to Baghdad, Iraq in 2003/2004. A story of dedication and sacrifice that almost no one knows. The unit served with honor and distinction being awarded,

Twelve Bronze Stars

Thirteen Purple Hearts

Ten Army Commendation Medals with "V" for Valor

The Valorous Unit Citation for consistent and repeated acts of bravery under fire during the year-long deployment

Made in the USA
Middletown, DE
27 February 2023

25403218R00139